Foreword

Blackberry Women takes the reader back to the 1930's Great Depression to lay open the turmoil and strife a Negro rural family endures. The scenes are unusual for many of us; but the boundless forces of nature control our lives, too, and compel us to follow the course we set for ourselves, however difficult the journey.

Who are the blackberry women we come to know after reading page after page in this novel? Dismal shadows are cast over these women, but you will recognize them as central characters who strongly desire love, respect, and prosperity in their daily lives. The constant search for who they are and what they hope to achieve depends upon the seasons of the year: warm springtime, long hot summer, lingering fall harvest, and bleak, cold winter.

Trifling social issues face each character, but the struggle for human values and self-esteem makes the search seem unending. The characters who suffer disabilities are constrained within the limitations of rural life. Those who escape are trapped in situations worse than what they start out with.

Blackberry Women reveals an image of the "great life" in developing urban cities, where flickering neon lights lure each character into poverty-stricken neighborhoods. The women who are left behind to wait for the harvest become more destitute, stymied by crop failure, family disruption, and financial hardship. Worse yet, *Blackberry Women* portrays a gloomy existence that clings to a single stand of hope, stretching across barren fields—without relevance.

But the novel is both relevant and successful. We learn that the turmoil the women endure totally stems from family disunity. The novel is successful, yet it allows tone to affect several historical situations that deprave women of the strength, courage, and bravery they are known for.

If you wish to know why Blackberry Women was written, compare the women in this novel with those in our modern society. It's a story of survival—plain and simple.

I. SABBATH MORN

Lola aroused minutes before daybreak from a night of deep slumber—so she thought. She jerked herself straight up in bed and tried to recall whether a dream or some weird noise had awakened her. Stretching her eyes wide open, she peered through the window across the hallway and saw that dawn was slowly erasing the darkness. Swinging her legs sideways out of bed, she gently tapped one foot on the floor, then the other one. Slowly she unfolded herself upward, hunched her shoulders, and stretched quietly. She sat back down on the bed and thought over again about the noise she either heard or dreamed about during the night. She

1

glanced sideways at Mirah lying on the other side of the bed and leaned over to listen to her breathing quietly in her sleep. "I don't want to awaken her," she thought. Unfolding herself upward again, Lola crept slowly toward the top of the stairs and listened for anyone who might be stirring within the household. She could feel the quiet stillness around her, except for the restful breathing of her older brothers and younger sisters sleeping in the other two rooms across the hallway. Descending the stairs, Lola paused after each step to listen again for sounds of anyone who might be stirring downstairs. Then she stood still at the bottom of the steps, careful not to make a sound.

Moving toward the front door, Lola pulled back the curtains and gazed through the transom window. Someone had hitched the mules to the wagon during the night, and she barely caught a glimpse of the mules trotting toward the gate, pulling the wagon behind them. By the time Lola realized that it was Papa in the wagon racing up the path, the mules and wagon turned onto the open road in front of the house and faded in the distance. "But who was the woman wearing a white bonnet and black cape sitting beside Papa in the wagon?" Lola wondered. Her cape rippled in the wind as the mules trotted up the path.

Letting the curtains silently slip from her fingers, Lola turned her head away from the window. At that moment, she knew that she hadn't been dreaming during the night. It was Papa she heard, but she couldn't think why he had gotten up before dawn on this Sunday morning.

Lola edged slowly along the narrow hallway. She opened each door she passed and stretched her neck to peer deeply inside. Nobody had slept in the two front rooms downstairs at all during the night; at least nothing had been disturbed.

She tried to reason why Papa awoke during the night and was just leaving the house as she awoke. But Lola still didn't know who was the strange lady seated beside Papa in the wagon. "Had the woman slept here during the night, or had Papa fetched her here?" She asked herself. Tiptoeing down the hallway and into the kitchen, she stopped suddenly when she reached Mama's bedroom door. She tried quietly to push the door open, but as it cracked slightly, a piercing screech stung the morning silence. Listening in the stillness, she cracked it wider as the smell of strong medicine and cleansing alcohol spread over her face and dared her to step inside the room. Her roving eyes rested on the hearth, where some wet rags were spread across the back of a chair to dry. A white washbowl sat on the floor full of clean water, waiting for someone to bathe. Lola wondered if Mama had been sick during the night.

Mama's bed was behind the door next to the wall. Lola pushed open the door wider against the bed and stretched her neck around it. Screech—the door sounded again, blasting throughout the house. Mama aroused from her deep silence. "What do you want, gal?" she groaned. Lola told Mama that she heard some noise downstairs before she got out of bed.

"Are you alright?" and "Where has Papa gone?" Lola asked. "Who was the lady wearing a black cape sitting beside Papa in the wagon?" Lola asked before Mama could answer her questions.

Without answering, Mama slowly peeled back the bed sheet. Before Lola's eyes appeared a tiny head covered with bronze, feisty curls. "You have another little baby sister," Mama said joyfully.

"Oh Mama, She's so tiny and pretty!" Lola said. "Can I hold her?" She leaned over and picked up the tiny baby. She wore a pretty little white gown no larger than those she had sewn for her own doll. She pressed her little sister close to her chest and kissed her precious, tiny head. Lola placed the nestling, squirming wee baby beneath Mama's breast and left the room to cook breakfast while Mama lay in bed with Lola's new baby sister. "It must have been the lady who helped Mama have her baby sitting beside Papa in the wagon," Lola convinced herself.

Sunday mornings are usually quiet, so no one hurries to get out of bed. "But I must hurry," Lola thought. Her mind was busy organizing the day's chores for her sisters and brothers. This morning was not like the others, since Mama had brought them a newborn baby. Lord knows Lola had known six other births, but none of them was quite like this one, with such ominous quietness creeping throughout the house. She shuttered to think that as soon as dawn spreads over the fields, her household would soon squelch the stillness she felt enveloping her.

There were the outside routine jobs at the barnyard to take care of, which Papa usually did on Sunday mornings; but he had taken home the woman who was helping Mama have her baby. Besides, he hardly slept at all during the night. Saturday night was a late night to bed for Lola's older brothers, so they had to be nudged from bed to get them moving to do Papa's work for him. Lola could hear footsteps, a snicker, and someone talking upstairs, but no one had come downstairs and stuck a head through the door. "I need to make a fire in the cook stove," Lola thought. "Then I will put on a kettle of water and make a pot of coffee." Lola knew that Papa would certainly want coffee to drink when he got back from down the road. She took the can off the pantry shelf and removed the lid. There was no coffee in the can! "What will Papa drink?" she wondered. Papa had been so anxiously awaiting the new baby that he forgot all about buying coffee. There certainly was no way for anyone to get to the store, except to walk, because Papa was using the only wagon they owned. To walk to the store and back would take all morning. "Oh dear," Lola whispered. "Papa will have to do without his coffee!" No sooner had Lola's disgust about the coffee left her than Mirah sauntered through the kitchen door.

"Why are you up so early, Lola?" Mirah asked.

"You have a brand-new baby sister, Mirah. Mama brought her to us last night," Lola replied, without looking up from the cook stove. "Go into Mama's room and see for yourself," she added.

Mirah was a trifling gal sometimes and didn't like to be questioned or told what to do when it came to working. Lola didn't want to spoil the morning fussing with Mirah, so she kept right on preparing breakfast, hardly looking up as she spoke. Mirah came back into the kitchen all in smiles. "What a pretty little baby," she said.

"Yes, Mirah, now we will have to help Mama care for her," Lola asserted.

The old black iron kettle sizzled on top the wood-burning cook stove. It gave Lola a signal that the stovetop was hot enough to begin frying the bacon and potatoes. She went out to the smoke house and pulled down a slab of bacon that Mama had already sliced from and headed back to the kitchen. Hurrying, she narrowly missed the top step in front of the kitchen door and stumbled into the kitchen, falling flat on her hands and knees. Quickly Lola jumped up and brushed herself off. She picked up the slab of bacon and laid it on the kitchen table. "No time to get hurt now," Lola thought. She sliced several pieces of bacon with the butcher knife and put them into the frying pan.

"What are you doing out there, Lola?" Mama asked.

"I'm cooking breakfast," Lola answered. "Mirah, please peel some potatoes so I can fry them after the bacon is done." Lola demanded. Mirah nodded her head approvingly and began peeling potatoes.

The bacon hadn't finished cooking, and Lola also had the biscuits to cook. She sifted enough flour for a big pan of biscuits and dumped some salt and baking powder into the flour. She also slapped a tablespoon of lard into the flour, added some buttermilk, and began kneading the dough. Afterwards, she separated the dough into little balls she flattened in the palm of her hand and placed them in the pan one by one. Moments later, she put the biscuits into the oven to bake.

Lola lifted each piece of bacon from the pan and threw the potatoes Mirah peeled into the same pan to fry, which splashed hot grease all over the stovetop. Mirah grabbed a top from the pantry to cover the potatoes and left them to smother in the frying pan. Then she returned the slab of bacon to the smokehouse.

Just about when the potatoes had smothered and the biscuits browned in the oven, Papa pulled up in the yard. He jumped out the wagon, tied the mules to the old hitching post out back, and walked into the kitchen. He was not much for conversation, and Lola knew this. Without asking questions about where he had been, she set a plate for him at the kitchen table and filled it with bacon, potatoes, and two hot biscuits. She hoped there would be enough for everyone to eat.

"Where's the coffee?" Papa asked.

"There's none here, Papa," Lola replied. "You'll have to do without coffee until someone goes to the store." Sitting himself down to eat, Papa hardly lifted his eyes from his plate. Lola prepared Mama's breakfast and took it to her where she lay with her new baby. Mirah prepared a place at the table for her sisters and brothers to eat their breakfast when they were ready, but she had to go upstairs and awaken them first. This morning her two brothers walked straight through the kitchen into the yard. They had to chop wood and feed the mules, hogs, and cattle before eating breakfast since Papa was awake nearly all night.

After the boys had finished eating, Lola's two younger sisters were to clean up the kitchen. Ginger will wash the dishes, and Greta will dry them and put the dishes in the cupboard. Lola and Mirah went upstairs to get ready for Sunday school. Ginger and Greta wanted also to go to Sunday school, but they decided to go to church later for the Children Day program after Sunday school. Besides, it gave them a few minutes to play with their new baby sister.

Lola's two oldest brothers left home soon after they turned sixteen years old. Russ went to work in the coal mines in West Virginia. Hugh went to work in the coal mines, too; but after a year went by, he left the mines and headed to the big industrial shipyard out east where ships the navy needed to help fight the war were being built. The farmland was producing hardly enough to keep her two oldest brothers alive, so they left home and found work elsewhere. Hugh promised Mama and Papa he would send money home to help with the farm; it never came. He hardly was able to care for himself in the big southeastern city. Living in shacks and rundown houses, Hugh quickly fell into a crime-infested ghetto life where vagrants, thieves, and criminals nestled.

Hugh, being the oldest child, was a sharp-eyed boy. His thick, black lips pushed way out beyond his nose, and his protruding forehead overshadowed his squinting hazel eyes. He was much too boyish, yet he was mature in his manner when helping Mama and Papa make decisions about the family.

Russ, too, was thick lipped. His smooth yellow skin stretched over his long bold forehead. His eyes were always relaxed, and they rested comfortably beneath his eyebrows. Both playful and rough at the same time, he loved teasing his sisters until he made them cry; and he wrestled with them as if they were all toys. Mama missed her boys when they left; and she never stopped worrying about each one of them, especially since she had heard from neither Hugh in the big city nor Russ in the coal mines a long way from home.

Van never liked playing and having fun with his brothers and sisters. He was much too serious for that. He kept his face twisted in a deep scowl, awaiting the scolding he never could take from Mama and Papa. If you looked at him, you knew immediately that he took the absence of his brothers deep within his heart when they left home. His lips were always rolled down; and his eyes were so tiny that they resembled two peas nestled in tiny pods, slow and sorrowful. He hardly ever smiled and sometimes would go the entire day without even speaking to anyone. He kept his thoughts to himself; and when anything unsavory was mentioned, he just walked away without even saying a word.

Ed was different. He talked and walked at the same time without even stopping to catch his breath. If anything happened, he quickened the pace as he talked. The top half of his body was much too large for his slim legs to support, but he stood tall and burley. His hair was kinked up on top of his head in tiny burrs; and when he combed his hair, the kinks went right back to the place where they had lain. Like the kinks on top his head, Ed was kinked-up, too. If anyone spoke to him, the expression on his face appeared in a frown as he cocked his head toward anyone who was speaking. Ed was born half deaf and hardly ever heard what anyone was saying to him, yet no one could understand what he was saying. It could have been a funny or sad thing spoken; Ed just never reacted to either one. When he did, you knew he hadn't heard a word of what was said. Like Van, he hardly ever laughed; instead, he kept a deep frown on his face that stretched across his black, smooth skin. His eyes were always the same—red and glaring, nearly popping out of their sockets whenever he spoke. He mumbled on and on to himself and became disgruntled whenever anyone spoke to him or asked him what he was talking about. Mama understood him, though, for she loved Ed and had more patience with him than she did with the other boys. She even cuddled him whenever she got the chance. Ed's sisters and brothers constantly yelled at him for fear he wouldn't hear what they were saying or whispered whenever ugly things were said to him.

Ed never attended school, so he learned what manners he had from watching how his brothers behaved. Mama taught him to read and write his name; for once he could write it, he was so proud of himself that he scrawled his name on every piece of paper he could find.

After his two older brothers left home, Ed had crying spells whenever he imagined that they would come to some terrible harm far away from home. He took the blame for his brothers leaving home personally, and it warped his whole mind and body. Sometimes Mama and Papa just looked at him and shook their heads in awe and pity.

Walden, a tender-hearted little boy, was barely past his second birthday when Hugh and Russ left home. He took to loving his other brothers, Van and Ed, and would never let them out of his sight. Whenever they went about the yard, barn, and field doing their work, Walden followed them; but they had difficulty chasing him back home. They were afraid that Walden would come to some danger. If they let Walden follow them, when they got tired of waiting for him to catch up while they walked ahead too fast, Van or Ed just scooped him up onto their shoulders and carried him; sometimes they ran, sometimes they walked, depending on how heavy Walden's weight felt on their shoulders. They tried spanking the little tyke and frightening him with scary stories, but nothing would discouraged Walden from following his brothers. Walden started following Van and Ed around the house and outdoors when he was hardly past two years old. Now that Walden was three, he obeyed his brothers; he went where they went and slept in the bed with them. He looked up to them as his playmates and best friends.

Being in their early teens, Van and Ed certainly did not want a little boy following them around lest he interrupted the many grown-up stories they shared with each other. They often hid from him or sneaked off when Walden fell asleep.

When nighttime came, Walden's brothers made him go to bed; but they had to make sure he was asleep before they wandered downstairs to join the other grown folks on the front porch, where they shared stories with visiting friends and neighbors.

When Walden was curious about what went on downstairs, he lay in bed, eyes wide open and barely moving, until Van and Ed returned and climbed into bed. Sometimes Van and Ed stayed overnight on Saturdays with friends and did not return home until late the next day.

Being a wide-eyed youngster, though, Walden knew exactly what to do the next time his brothers sneaked out of bed at night and didn't take him with them. He would get out of bed and slowly creep unnoticed behind Van and Ed so he could see what they were doing downstairs and where they were going.

Seeing his brothers just as they stepped out the room, Walden crept behind Van and Ed quietly at a safe distance so that he would not be noticed. He kept watching and following his brothers as they went outdoors and into the back yard. In his childish mind, Walden felt safe and sure of himself that he could follow his brothers unnoticed. As he stepped out the door and crawled down the steps into the yard, he could see the dim view of the two boys as they disappeared into the night. Standing there frightened and stunned in his tracks in the darkness, Walden could no longer see where he was going.

He continued groping in the dark and feeling his way inch by inch. He just kept searching; but when he heard the mules making some weird noise, he ducked inside the outhouse at the corner of the woodpile so his brothers wouldn't see him. He became so confused, he hardly recognized where he was. As soon as he got inside the outhouse, he started to find out a little bit more about what was this place he had stumbled into. He climbed on top the toilet seat, felt around the top edges for a while, and was surprised to discover a round hole large enough to fit his head into. "This is a good place to hide so no one will find me," he thought. Groping for his balance—swish! Walden plunged into the dark hole and sank to the bottom, smothered in a sticky, murky, stinky slush.

Well—when dawn slowly unfurled, everyone in the household was shocked to discover that Walden had disappeared during the night without even a trace! When he could not be found in bed, Mama was certain that Van and Ed had taken Walden with them when they visited their friends overnight. As the day wore on, Mama waited patiently until Van and Ed returned.

"Where is your baby brother Walden?" Mama asked.

"We left him in bed because we did not leave until after dark," Van replied.

"But he is not here!" Mama cried. "What have you done with him?"

All afternoon and evening as the hours dragged on, the boys sank deep into horror to think they were guilty of Walden's disappearance. They searched frantically under the house and in the woods at the edge of the field but turned up no trace of Walden. The search kept up for a week, silently. Still they could not find Walden. Feeling responsible for his loss, Van and Ed fell into such deep, soul-wrenching grief that they were unable to utter a sound to anyone the entire week. They just sat around the house mourning their brother's loss in agony, pain, and shock. The memory alone was just too horrible to bear for fear someone else in the family would also disappear.

There was no remembrance of poor little Walden—just silence and grief. No one reported the child missing—he just disappeared. Whenever anyone asked about Walden's whereabouts, with guilt and shame spread over their faces, they lied to them saying, "Gypsies stole him." His brothers were too ashamed to question whether or not the truth was being told. Scary ideas crept into their minds whenever they thought about poor Walden.

Deep within Mama's heart, she knew what had happened to her child; but she remained silent because her heart had shredded into pain, melted, and spread all over her chest. Walden's disappearance simply was not discussed in the neighborhood, at church, or in the household among family members. Papa promised to board up that old outhouse. His grief was so overbearing that he would never let this incident happen again. Van never returned to school for fear someone would ask about his little lost brother or see the guilt lying bare on his sad face. He had only gotten as far as the sixth grade, but he knew it was time for him to quit.

Ginger and Greta were best-of-friend sisters. Nothing could keep them from sharing all their secrets and competing with each other. They, too, were partly deaf, so they naturally found similarities between themselves. They could talk to each other in a language unknown to their sisters and brothers, especially when they did not want anyone to know what they knew. If you asked Ginger or Greta what they were saying, hardly ever did they understand the question. Mirah constantly nagged at her sisters, seeking to make sense out of whatever they talked about.

Ginger was a stubborn girl who got riled up at the least unfavorable look anyone gave her. She had a pleasant face, but she loved to roll her eyes in a threatening way at the thought of her sisters being unkind to her. Behind every threat, she picked up various small objects available to her and hurled them angrily toward her sisters.

Mama and Papa took Ginger to the doctor as soon as they discovered that she was not responding when they spoke to her. The doctor told them that the child had been born with a disease or that she had contacted rheumatic fever shortly after she was born, and it left her partially deaf. Because of her deafness, she was unable to pronounce her words properly and clearly. No one asked them why Ginger was partially deaf, so Mama and Papa never took her to the doctor again for a follow-up. When their next child Greta was born with a hearing loss, Mama thought that the child had gotten the same disease that her sister Ginger and her brother Ed probably had.

Ginger and Greta suffered through many days when they sat in their school classes without hearing or learning anything the teacher talked about. They just sat in the dummy corner because of it and did not understand the lessons either, so they had to strain their ears to hear whenever anything was being taught. They tried to read the lessons from the book; but not being able to say the words correctly left them at a loss when learning how to read, write, or add simple figures. The school children thought they were odd. When they asked other children to explain the lesson to them, no one bothered to take the time. Mostly, Ginger and Greta just played softball at recess or raced against the other children to see who could run the fastest. Ginger especially was chosen to manage and supervise the recreational activities for the school children.   Often she was both referee and score keeper during the Saturday softball games.

Greta was a little taller than her sister Ginger, although Ginger was older. She walked with an air of vain arrogance and made everybody's troubles her own. Greta had a heart that was made of love and kindness. When her sisters or anyone else took advantage of her goodness, they often would snicker at her when she did not speak distinctly and clearly, pretending she lacked good sense. It hurt her when that happened, but she always returned such meanness with kindness. Her sisters were hardly ever kind to her as well, so Greta rested on the edge of everyone's feelings. She didn't even realize that she was illiterate and had no under-standing why she could not get book learning.

Greta's love for Mama had no boundary, and Mama loved her, too. They were like sisters, she and her mama; nothing came between them. If one of Greta's sisters as much as rolled her eyes at Mama, she ran and told Mama, seeking to win her favor. Greta expected favors and usually got them from Mama, such as holding her hand, walking beside Mama, or carrying her pocketbook whenever they were walking. She loved to hug Mama and comb her hair. She especially wanted Mama's attention when she had figured out how to solve a difficult task such as showing Mama how well she could cook or iron a pretty dress. As a reward, Mama protected and cuddled Greta and wanted no harm to come to her as she grew up. Although her sisters were often cruel to both Ginger and Greta, Mama talked to them constantly about their sisters' disability and told them that they were not able to understand simple words and expressions the way they did. Greta admired her new baby sister, but she was determined not to let another baby get in the way of her love for Mama she openly showed. Greta wanted to care for Mama and her new baby. She loved her new baby sister so much that she asked Mama if she could stay home from school when fall comes to help her raise the new baby.

The two deaf sisters never knew anything but a hard day's work on the farm, and they tried to win favors from the family through their long hours of work. They even boasted about who could pick more pounds of cotton or chop the fastest peanut row, while racing to win the contest. The back-breaking strain of the cotton picking kept them tired and irritable most of the time. Besides, the burdens of the whole family rested upon the backs of Ginger and Greta.

Whenever outside hired hands were needed, they were the ones chosen to go. They worked on the farm from sunup to dusk for fifty cents per day; only the adults made seventy-five cents. If they came home before quitting time, they were scolded and driven back to work until sunset. No one admired them for the hard work they did; instead, they became the workhorses of the family. The two girls were only concerned about letting Mama and Papa know that the labor was hard, and they always did the work no one else wanted to do. They thought it was what they were supposed to do, since farm work was all they were good at doing.

So here was Sunday morning and the two deaf sisters were cleaning up the dirty dishes the family had left in the kitchen. They didn't mind doing the dishwashing, though, because they ate as much as they wanted without being under the watchful eyes of Lola and Mirah, who were busy getting ready for Sunday school. They would be left to take matters into their own hands, especially making preparations for boiling the vegetables, frying the chicken, or baking the ham for dinner.

Nita and Gaye, Mama and Papa's two youngest girls before the baby was born, were fast buddies and played with each other constantly until Nita became a troublemaker. Nita was a year and a half older than Gaye, though, but Gaye thought she was older, much too old for a baby sister. Whenever they argued, they could find the ugliest names to hurl at each other like silly, stupid, or crazy. Gaye called Nita "plump" whenever she became angry with her, and that threw them into a viscous fistfight. Nita always sent Gaye to Mama screaming, crying, and yelling, so Nita called her "tattletale." Each one of her sisters wondered why Nita did such ugly things to Gaye that kept her running to Mama, telling tales about being slapped, hit, and called ugly names; but Nita kept right on doing it.

Nita was disobedient at an early age and all during her childhood. She would not listen to Mama. When she was barely six years old, she had gotten into the habit of sneaking off alone to ramble in Mama's room among her secrets that she kept in a safe place. When she thought everyone was out of sight, and her sister Gaye was not watching her, Nita wandered off in search of mischievous behavior.

One day just after Nita had been left alone on her promise of good behavior, she waited patiently until Mama and the girls had left for the cotton field before she started roving over the house looking for something to meddle with. She wandered into Mama's room, closed the door behind her so Gaye couldn't find her, and started examining what was hidden in the huge trunk at the foot of Mama's bed. After she had drug all the clothes and other items on the floor, Nita crawled on her hands and knees onto the fireplace hearth and began to rake among the ashes. She wanted to find out what those ashes were and what was hidden underneath them. Feeling the warm ashes, she poked her little fingers further into some hot cinders and burned her left thumb to a nub and badly blistered her forefinger. Nita let out such a chilling scream beyond the household and edge of the cotton field that it sent Mirah scrambling to the house to find out what was the problem. She threw open the door to Mama's room and found Nita sitting on the hearth holding her burnt fingers on her lap and squalling as loud as she could. Mirah took Nita in her arms and ran back to the cotton field to tell Mama that Nita had burned her fingers raking in the hot ashes and cinders in the fireplace. Mama tore a rag off the bottom of her skirt and bandaged the child's blistering fingers. She grabbed Nita from Mirah's arms, while the child sniffled and cried in pain, and ran toward the house as fast as she could.

Flying into the house, Mama cuddled Nita closely, laid her on the bed, and tried to make her comfortable. Then she made a salve out of lard and alcohol and rubbed it on Nita's fingers. It soothed the pain a little, but Nita continued to sob throughout the afternoon. "The pain has not stopped yet," Mama thought. She stayed with Nita until late in the evening when she fell asleep in Mama's bed.

Nita's sisters took to calling her "Nubs" after this terribly painful burning accident happened. They all pretended it was funny, but it only reminded Nita of the pain she felt when she burned her fingers. Mama was both angry and sad that Nita had gotten burned. Mostly she was disappointed that Nita disobeyed her and went into her room to ramble when she had been scolded for it time and time again. The burned fingers healed well; even so, an ugly scar was left on both her thumb and forefinger. Nita kept those two fingers tucked beneath the others, and she never let anyone see her hand or talked to anyone about the terrible accident. The mere mentioning of "nubs" brought tears to Nita's eyes whenever she remembered how painful the experience had been.

Gaye felt sorry for Nita most of the time after she burned her fingers, but not for long. Regardless of which side was winning, whether in games, teasing, or arguing, Gaye was always on the side of the winner. Hardly ever did she like being a loser in any kind of competition. She was a pretty, brown child, with long, black, curly plaits. Actually, she was Mama's cute little girl until her baby sister came along. Now she would be pushed aside to grow up. Gaye learned to stay away from Nita, though, for she often got into too much trouble following Nita and her older sisters.

The minute Nita and Gay ran downstairs this Sunday morning, Nita drug Gaye into Mama's room because Nita knew she was not allowed in there. They tiptoed into the bedroom to see if Mama was there and were surprised to see her lying in bed with a new baby. Gaye jumped into the bed with

Mama and stared into the baby's face and kissed her on the cheek. Nita followed Gaye and jumped into the bed, too, and landed on the other side of Mama and the baby. Mama was stressed now, knowing that Gaye was very quick and agile and that Nita was just too rough with her younger sister, let alone the new baby.

Nita and Gaye both watched as the baby guzzled milk underneath the bed sheet from Mama's breast, slurping with each swallow. Suddenly Nita pulled the sheet from the baby's head to kiss her. "Get away from here!" Mama scolded, fearing Nita would sit on the baby and crush her tiny body. Nita just stared into the baby's face and called her a little wiggle worm all wrapped up under the sheet.

Mama was fearful that Nita and Gaye would crawl on the baby, so she hollered for Greta to get the children out of the room and fix something for them to eat. They were so hungry, that at the least mention of food, the two of them scrambled off the bed to the floor and ran into the kitchen. There they found a cup of milk, hot buttered biscuits, and fried potatoes awaiting them. They gobbled the food down in a hurry and raced to the front yard to play their favorite game, hide-and-go-seek. When they got tired, they sat beside the chimney and made mud pies in the dirt until it was time for them to eat their dinner.

Lola and Mirah bounded down the stairs, all decked out in their pretty dresses and Sunday shoes, ready for the long trek to Sunday school. As they turned the corner and headed down the steps, Ginger and Greta met them and fussed about how pretty they looked. "We come to church later," Greta said, and Ginger nodded her head to approve what Greta said. They finished breakfast dishes and started the vegetables cooking. By the time they leave home for the Children Day program, part of the dinner will have cooked.

Lola and Mirah stuck their heads inside the door to Mama's room and whispered to her that they were leaving for Sunday school. "Be good girls in Sunday school, and come straight home when the Children Day program is over," Mama cautioned. "Mirah, don't forget it's your turn to set the table for dinner," Mama added.

"Yes, Mama," Mirah answered. Mama stretched her neck toward the window, and after seeing Lola and Mirah passing by, she lay back down in bed, snuggling her baby closer to her breast.

With a flash Mira and Lola were out of the yard and heading down the path toward the road. No sooner were they off the dirt path leading to the graveled road than Lola and Mirah began to walk faster. They had over two miles to walk and did not want to be late for Sunday school although they always most nearly were.   Lola walked somewhat slower than Mirah, but not for long. Mirah grabbed her by the hand and started pulling her along so she could keep up and wouldn't lag so far behind. Lola knew that if she walked too fast, she would start sweating and ruin her pretty dress. Besides, she didn't want to be untidy when she got to Sunday school. Nevertheless, Mirah kept tugging Lola along so she could keep up with her.

"Mama will scold us both when we get home if we are late for Sunday school," Mirah warned.

They walked on down the hill past Mr. Kraft's shabby farmhouse, their nearest neighbor. He was much too old to go to church; besides, he had no way of getting there. Mr. Kraft waved to them as they hurried past his house. "Don't be late for Sunday school and behave yourselves, too," he yelled from the porch. They paid him no attention and didn't answer back; they just walked hurriedly on toward the church.

Next they passed the Green's house. It was painted a dark-brown, dull color with white trimming and built with vertical side boards. It was a cute house, though, sitting in the field facing the road, boasting a neat white fence and flower garden on the inside of it. Mrs. Green took a lot of pride in her flower garden; and when the flowers were in full bloom, she welcomed anyone who wandered up the path to see them close-up. Lola and Mirah had walked past so many times, they dared not look at the pretty flowers; they were afraid that a simple glance would make them stare too long and hard at the quaint house and flowers. They had no time to lose and must hurry along. Besides, Mr. Green had let the cows out to graze in the pasture across the road, and they were trotting down the path toward them while trying to cross over into the pasture. Lola and Mirah were afraid of the cows, so they stepped up their pace and ran part the way toward the church so the cows wouldn't cross in front of them. They hid their fear of the cows and wouldn't tell Mama; had Mama known they were afraid, she would not have let them walk to Sunday school.

It was difficult passing the only country store in the area as Lola and Mirah walked further down the road. Mrs. Vant, who owned the country store, had stuff to sell that lured nearly all the children in the neighborhood. Lola and Mirah wanted to stop in there and buy a five-cent soda pop or a penny sucker, but today, they must hurry on. Besides, they each had only a nickel and a few pennies to put in the Sunday school collection. Mrs. Vant's store was always nice and cool in the summer, having the only huge fan in the neighborhood, and warm and cozy in the winter. Children always wanted to stay longer than they were supposed to. They liked standing in front of the huge fan that sat in the corner of the store in the summertime, letting the cool breeze sweep over their faces and dresses. Then they wished for the racks and racks of clothes and the pots, pans, and dishes loaded on the shelves. Cookies, candy, and other sweets in the store cases made them drool to look at and delicious to taste. If Lola and Mirah weren't in a hurry, they would stop in just to feel some of the cool fresh air escaping from the fan, but Mama had warned them enough times not to stop at the store and spend their nickels Papa gave them for Sunday school. Today, they knew better than to stop. They walked past the white gate posts leading to the store and never as much as said a word to each other about stopping to buy something. When church was over, the store had closed for the evening.

Somewhere in the distance, Lola and Mirah heard the church bell ringing. The tall spiral steeple atop the church roof leaped out above the trees and welcomed them as they passed a thick grove of bushes spreading toward a clearing on the road. They knew instantly that they would soon be on the pathway leading to the church door.

Just as Lola and Mirah climbed up the steps to the church, Superintendent Frigs grabbed the door, pulled it wide open, and pushed them inside. "You're just in time," he said, and he closed the door quietly behind them.

As Lola and Mirah entered the church, the Sunday school children were singing "Glory to His Name." Lola and Mirah took their places in a pew near their favorite girl friends. Then a prayer was led, with more joyful singing, and everyone tuned in with their glorious voices. The introduction to the lesson with comments from the Sunday school teacher was well underway before Lola began to listen to the teacher. She kept talking, whispering, and meddling with the other children. Mirah nudged her several times in the side before she paid attention to what the teacher was saying. Also, Lola had all the other children's eyes on her. In her own boastful way, she knew they were looking at a pretty girl wearing a cute dress.

Finally, it was time to be dismissed from Sunday school classes. Mirah was not in Lola's class, so they separated until it was time for the Children Day program. Mirah's teacher was very stern and somewhat serious about the Bible stories and the impression they made on the young teenagers who were studying the Bible. In less than ten minutes, the teacher had previewed the lesson and was starting to ask questions about what she had discussed in the Bible stories. No one raised a hand, and Mirah was hoping that she wouldn't be called on to answer any questions. Not so! She was called on just as the door burst wide open and in walked the girl who was taking attendance and collecting the Sunday school money for the weekly report. Mirah hoped by the time the girl leaves, no one will have noticed that she had not studied her lesson for today, as her teacher had plainly instructed her to do last Sunday. Mirah sat there quietly, unable to answer any questions. After hesitating for what seemed like two minutes, the teacher called on the next child for the answer. Mirah felt guilty that she did not know the answer to the teacher's question. She tried to tell the teacher that the reason she had not studied was because there was a new baby in her family. The teacher paid her no attention, so Mirah became stunned and saddened when she was not given the chance to tell her Sunday school class how beautiful their new baby was.

As soon as Sunday school was dismissed, the children were all ushered into the church vestibule to assemble for the Children Day program. One by one the boys and girls took their places in the pew with their own classes. Then the program started with each child giving a religious recitation. They quoted Bible verses, recited poems, or sung choir songs.

Ginger and Greta arrived at the church just in time for the Children Day program. They would not be reciting a Bible verse or singing a song. Whenever they said a Bible verse in church, it was a very short one like "Jesus Wept" because the children couldn't understand what they were saying. When they were on a program before and said their lines, the children laughed and snickered at them when their speeches were not spoken clearly. Besides, they could not hear their names called and had to rely on the other children to tell them when the time came for their speech. The incident often left Ginger and Greta in tears, so they never tried speaking at church in front of the other children again.

Today was no different. They just sat there enjoying the other children and stretching their heads to one side, trying their best to hear the songs and speeches. No one noticed them, so they just joined in with the other children and clapped their hands when they clapped theirs.

When Lola was called on for her recitation, all the color drained from her face. She had not known that her shyness would cause her to panic. When she had gotten just one line recited, the rest of her verse drifted away and hid behind the faces of all those children staring wide-eyed at her. Finally, without remembering the rest of her lines, Lola returned to her seat and sat down as snuffed snickers went wild among the children. She was too brokenhearted to even lift her head. She covered her face in shame and wanted no one to see the briny tears that trickled down her cheeks. The program continued on, but it was not until the next two children had spoken their parts when Lola sat up and listened to the rest of the program. She hoped the teacher would give her a second chance to say her recitation, but there was no time left at the end of the program.

All the children looked forward to the refreshments after the Children Day program was over. Their moms, aunts, and sisters fried some chicken, and baked pound cakes and cookies. Their papas and uncles made the yearly big brown wooden barrel of fresh lemonade. They stirred it with a long, wooden ladle after all the huge bags of sugar had been dumped into the barrel and mixed with the lemons. Then five ten gallon buckets of cold water were added until the mixture turned syrupy sweet. Finally, three or four blocks of ice were carefully placed into the barrel and stirred some more until the lemonade was ice-cold and tasted just right.

One by one the children took their places in the line, holding a white paper cup and plate in their hands. The cup was filled to the brim with lemonade, and the plate was piled with fried chicken, light bread, cake, and cookies. They walked over to the tin-roof shed underneath a shade tree and sat on the long bench that stretched from one end of the shade to the other. They ate their chicken, cookies, and cake. Then they drank the ice-cold lemonade overflowing in each cup, which they loved best of all.

All the children, except Lola, ate and drank the refreshments they had been served. She left her plate at the table and scurried around looking for Mirah. She saw Ginger and Greta sitting together, but she didn't see Mirah. Lola ran around the outside of the church and searched inside behind each pew, where Mirah and her friends liked to play while everyone else was eating and where no one would notice them.

When Mirah went outside the church, she did not see her sisters. She left, walking alone, thinking they had gone home and left her behind. Just as Lola looked out the front door of the church, she saw Mirah heading down the path toward home. Lola remembered that she had not eaten and drunk her lemonade with the other children. She went over to where Ginger and Greta were sitting and told them Mirah had left without them and that it was time to go home. Remembering again that she had not eaten, Lola decided to take her cake and lemonade home to Mama so she could have something to eat and a cool drink, too.

Half walking and half running to catch up with Mirah, they hurried down the road back home. Lola hoped the sun would not melt the ice in Mama's lemonade. Each time she stumbled on a rock in the road or changed the cup of lemonade to her other hand, she spilled it bit by bit; but she would not let her sisters Ginger and Greta help her carry the cup of lemonade, since Ginger had already dropped the cake in the dirt while trying to keep up with Lola. She left the cake lying in the dirt, thinking the ants would eat it. Feeling sad, they walked on, hoping Mama wouldn't mind that Ginger dropped the cake Lola was bringing her.

The dry summer heat evaporated half of the cup of lemonade and melted the ice, yet they had another half mile to walk. By the time Lola started down the path toward the house, she barely had a third of a cup of lemonade left to take Mama, squeezing it tighter and tighter in her hand. She thought about Mama bringing them a baby sister, so she knew Mama would still be in bed. Without stopping to rest on the steps after the long walk home from church, she raced into Mama's room with the cup containing two or three ounces of warm lemonade. "Here, Mama, I brought you and the baby some lemonade." Lola said. Mama placed the cup on her dry lips and took one swallow.

"Thank you, my child," Mama said. "Your mama is very thirsty, and this lemonade is just what I want." Mama told Lola that she was very proud of her because she walked a long time, and still a big sip was in the cup. "While you were gone, I named your new sister 'B r o w n e s e' for her brown skin, bronze curls, and beautiful brown eyes," Mama exclaimed."

"That's a pretty name," Lola replied. She ran out the door yelling "The baby's name is Brownese."

"What a pretty name," her sisters said all at once as Lola raced down the hallway announcing the news. She was excited because she was the first one to tell her sisters the name of their new baby. "Mama named our new sister Brownese!" Lola repeated. The girls all rushed into Mama's room and told her how excited they were about the name of their new sister.

Lola and Mirah were the first to change their clothes and hang them up until next Sunday, when they will wear them to Sunday school again. Then they went downstairs to set the table and warm up the food for the Sunday evening's dinner. Mirah went upstairs and yelled to Ginger and Greta to change clothes before dinner. A place was set for everyone at the table, but only Papa and the girls would be sitting at the table for dinner. Mama had not gotten out of bed after the birth of the new baby. Van and Ed were off running around the country-side, visiting their friends, and would not be home at dinnertime. On Sundays they stayed out as late as possible, grabbed a bite to eat and barely made it to bed in time to get two or three hours of sleep before daybreak. Usually they got up on weekday mornings before dawn to begin plowing the long rows of cotton and peanuts.

The aroma of food warming on the stove and the hot bread rolls baking in the oven drifted through the house and alerted the girls that it was dinnertime. Papa, who was the last to arrive, took his place at the head of the table. He barely had blessed the food before the girls at the table were serving themselves and starting to eat. Lola pre-pared Mama's dinner and took it to her room. Then she came back and sat down at Mama's place at the table. Nita and Gaye scrambled in from an afternoon of playing in the yard. "Look at your hands and face!" Mirah scolded. "Go wash them and don't eat a mouthful until you have cleaned yourselves up."

Greta noticed that Lola had taken Mama's place at the table and quickly began to show her hurt feelings. She teasingly told everyone at the table that Lola forgot what to say when it was her turn to say a recitation at the church. Ginger joined in and told how Lola tried to bring home a cup of lemonade for Mama, but she had nearly spilled all of it before she got home. "Tell how you dropped the cake in the dirt, Ginger," Lola replied, angrily. They all laughed when Lola said that. Papa could foresee trouble creeping up at the table, so he quickly spoke up and changed the subject.

"Let's eat, and quit teasing," Papa said. He picked up the dish of cabbage, which no one liked, and handed it to Mirah, who was busy trying to get Nita and Gaye to eat their dinner, like big girls, without spilling any on the floor. They had already eaten their bread rolls when Papa warned them again, "Eat your dinner, girls, and cut out the playing at the table!"

Before Papa could get the words out of his mouth, Nita was coughing and choking on a piece of bread that had lodged in her throat. Hacking and straining to clear her throat, the piece of bread flew from her mouth and landed in Papa's plate. "That's it! Leave the table now!" Papa screamed at Nita. Poor Nita, coughing and sobbing at the same time, had barely started to eat, but now she had to wait until everyone finished eating before she could return to the table.

After that incident, the girls sat silently and finished eating. Nita returned to the table, sorry for what she had done, and finished eating her dinner. Gaye was the last to leave the table, so she will help in the kitchen to clean up the dishes. Ginger was the person in charge of washing the dishes this week. Greta was to dry the dishes; but today,

Nita would help them, too, because she had been sent from the table.

Gaye was a tiny, frail child. She stood on a stool and took the dishes from Ginger after she washed them in the pan of hot, sudsy dishwater. Then Gaye placed the soapy dishes in a pan of hot rinse water. Greta took them out of the rinse water and dried them with the white dish towel that Mama bleached from flour sacks. Nita placed the dishes in the cupboard and took a wet rag and wiped the tablecloth clear of the crumbs that were scattered. When the dishes had all been washed and put away, Greta swept the kitchen and dining room floors.

The four girls raced at once to the front porch to listen to Lola and Mirah's tales and to watch the cars on the road go by. Quickly they joined in on the fun and laughter they had with one another during the day and took turns telling funny stories. Papa took his place in Mama's room, where they chatted for a couple of hours. After darkness fell, each child yelled good night to Mama and Papa and trudged upstairs to bed.

Sometime after midnight, a car door slammed in the distance. It had dropped Van and Ed off at the top of the path. After about five minutes, Van and Ed stumbled into the kitchen. Before going upstairs to bed, they stopped momentarily to open the cook stove oven and grab a piece of fried chicken left over from dinner. Before Van could swallow the first mouthful, Papa bounded into the kitchen and warned the boys about arriving home so late on Sunday night. "You are not allowed to eat in this house after midnight," Papa scolded. "Get your hands off of that chicken and hurry up to bed so you can get a fresh start in the morning plowing the field," he snarled. Without turning their heads, the boys trampled out of the kitchen, and went upstairs to bed. The door was closed behind them, and they settled down for the night. Lying there quietly breathing, Van strained to listen for any signs of Papa snoring during the night. If he heard him snoring, he wondered if he could sneak back downstairs to fetch that piece of chicken he started to eat without disturbing Papa. He heard cars on the road passing by, dogs barking on the next farm, and owls hooting mournful cries. Finally he fell asleep, dreading the hard labor facing him at daybreak. The only thing he hated about this night was that he was too lazy and sleepy to sneak back downstairs to finish that piece of fried chicken he had started to eat. "The chicken will have to wait until dawn," Van thought.

Except for the noise the boys made when they came in around midnight, the household slept quietly throughout the night. They will awaken at dawn to greet a grueling workday under the hot, broiling summer sun.

II. CURSE THE DAWN

As soon as dawn split the heavens, Papa went up-stairs, yelling at anyone within the sound of his voice to get up instantly. Knowing the boys stirred lazily in the mornings, he didn't hesitate to call each one by name: "Van, Ed, get up! It's time to go to work!" Van was sorry he stayed out later than he should have. If Papa knew how sleepy Van was, Papa would boot his butt out of bed. Most of the time, Van and Ed were obedient and got home early on Sunday nights.

Papa waited silently for each one sleeping to answer before he yelled the names of the other children. Unable to get a response from the lazy boys, Papa went to their bed first. He yanked at the wrinkled sheet coiled around Van's body, grabbed it angrily, and rolled Van into it. As Papa tugged on the sheet, he dragged Van out of bed onto the floor. Van angrily cursed the dawn and Papa, too. "You and Ed get up from here! It's time to go to work," Papa begged. Van picked himself up off the floor while Ed stumbled out of bed, following behind Van. Pacing themselves as slowly as possible, they put their clothes on and went downstairs to feed the barnyard animals.

The girls in the next room got out of bed as soon as they heard the loud commotion coming from the boys' room. They usually awoke each other and made sure no one got more sleep than the other one did. Mama taught the girls that as soon as they got out of bed, they were to make them up and tidy the rooms before coming downstairs. Lola and Mirah usually cooked breakfast while Ginger and Greta milked the cows and gathered from the garden vegetables that were to be prepared for dinner and supper.

Nothing ever changed on the farm. In the early-thirties, the routine was getting up at dawn, going to the field, returning late in the evening, cooking and eating supper, and getting to bed on time.

Long before Papa awoke Van and Ed, he had gone to the stables and fed the mules. Papa was a good farmer, and he loved those mules the same way he loved tilling the soil. He made the boys take good care of the animals and respect them, too, because the mules were a great source of strength and the cows and hogs kept the family alive.

As soon as Ginger and Greta finished milking the cows, Van and Ed fed them and let them out to graze in the pasture and soak up the morning sun. They needed to feed the hogs and pigs as well, so they shucked some corn and gathered raw vegetables to take to the pigpen. The pigs squealed and grunted as if they were starving, as they usually were, and almost grabbed their food from the boys' hands before they could release it into the trough. They started to squeal some more, anxious to devour each morsel left in the trough. When the grunting and squealing stopped, the boys were sure they had gotten enough to eat.

Then Van and Ed wandered off to the wood-pile to gather up and chop wood to make a fire underneath the round three-legged black pot on the woodpile in the back yard. Afterwards, they filled it with cold water drawn from the pump.

When the mules finished eating, Papa led Lucy, his favorite mule, to the wagon and hitched her up. Ed jumped on the back of the other mule, Ginny, and rode her to the wagon so Papa could hitch her beside Lucy. Papa needed these two mules to pull the wagon to the back gate farm. He gathered the plows and plow blades used to cultivate the peanut crop, and the boys dumped them into the wagon. Next they loaded the hoes that each girl and Ed would need to chop cotton and files to sharpen them with. Hoes would not cut wire grass that was taking over young plants unless they were keenly sharpened. After using them to shave three or four rows of twisting, tough wire grass, the hoes became dull and needed filing again.

Papa knew exactly how he wanted the mules hitched, not too tight and not too loose, for he had done this job over and over throughout the years and was not about to let the boys try. Their job was to carry small objects to the wagon and load them along with the heavy plows.

When Papa left the hitching job for the boys to do, Lucy and Ginny had trouble with their gait. If the reins were too tight, they dug the ground with their forefeet; they pitched and reared and would not pull the heavy load of farm equipment piled into the wagon.

First, Papa puts a chain mouth bit in Lucy's mouth, then in Ginny's. The bit guides the mules on the path and helps them to walk in the direction the driver steers. The bits are equipped with blinders on each side, which keep the mules from being distracted by unfamiliar objects. Second, Papa places a collar on each mule and runs long leather straps through a series of loops and fasteners attached to each collar. Next, the mules are strapped to the wagon tongue between them, which keeps the team moving at an even gait as they pull the loaded wagon. Afterwards, Papa attaches Lucy and Ginny to a single tree that hangs from the front end of the wagon. Finally, he places the reins in the buckboard until he is ready to take the wagon to the field.

Stepping into the wagon, Papa calmed the mules, tightened the reins, and held them firmly in his grip. Then he guided the mules and wagon toward the house and fastened them loosely to the hitching post. Quickly he lit to the ground and headed toward the kitchen, where his breakfast awaited him. Walking up the steps to the porch and before entering the kitchen door, Papa turned to glimpse Van and Ed walking from the barn toward the edge of the yard. No sooner had they reached the mules tied to the hitching post than Ed let out a taunting, shrilling whistle at Lucy and Ginny. The noise frightened and spooked both the mules into such frenzy that it sent them pitching and jump-ing out of control. Papa was barely able to leap from the porch and jump into the wagon to grab the reins just as the mules started to run wildly toward the open field. He stood up in the wagon and pulled the reins back hard; but on they raced, while all the farm equipment loaded on the wagon flew every which-a-way. The mules had a running start that made it impossible to stop them instantly from racing to the edge of the field toward the woods, and Ginny, being so stubborn, just kept charging on. Now, they were trotting faster, wagon trailing behind them, with Papa leaning back on the reins in the middle of the wagon and yelling at the top of his voice "Whoa Lucy, Whoa Ginny!" Papa calmed the mules slowly and drove them back to the house. This time he tied them more securely to the post.

Then he faced Van and Ed, who had wandered into the kitchen and sat down to eat breakfast. With an ugly growl, Papa gave Ed a tongue lashing for the problem he caused, even before they could get to work. The two boys sat there stunned, never taking their glaring eyes off Papa and too afraid to open their mouths. Ed gathered enough nerve to mumble "damn mules" and a string of curse words underneath his breath. Papa's eyes met Ed's at the same time his hand lashed across Ed's face, leaving him too ashamed to even speak. Ed jumped up from the table and ran into the yard bellowing and crying. "I'm leaving home tonight and never coming back to work on the farm," he yelled. Ed sat under the tree by the fence until the girls who were going to the field finished eating before he was allowed to go into the kitchen and eat the rest of his breakfast left on his plate. Papa sat down to eat his breakfast without saying another word to either of the boys.

Noticing Papa moving toward the wagon, Ed thought about the ruckus he caused, the ugly whistle at the mules, and the way he talked back to Papa. Cautiously, Ed moved toward the wagon and waited motionless aside while Van and Papa reloaded the plows and other equipment that flew from the wagon as it sailed across the field. Ed inched closer and closer toward the wagon, ready to jump in as soon as Papa motioned him to do so.

When he did, Ed Jumped up and down as high as he could. He sat on the edge of the wagon and promised Papa that he would behave himself the rest of the day. Ed was happy that he was allowed to ride in the wagon to the field across the narrow creek.

Ginger pumped two one gallon pails of cool water from the well to carry to the field. The workers will use one pail of water for a fresh, cool drink during the morning hours. The other pail of water will be let down into the spring at the edge of the creek to keep cool for drinking during noon lunch and the rest of the afternoon, for they will not be returning home until early evening.

Lola was mindful to prepare lunch for the family to take to the field since she was staying home today. First she set a pan of biscuits, some slices of fatback, and boiled white potatoes and cabbage on the table. Next, she placed the boiled vegetables and meat together in an enamel pan and set the pan inside the basket. Then she wrapped some biscuits in a dishtowel and put them into the big straw basket next to the enamel pan. Lastly, she put forks into the basket to eat with.

Waving good-bye to Mama and leaving her behind to care for little Brownese, Mirah and Ginger grabbed their straw hats and got into the wagon. Seeing the wagon was ready to leave, Greta grabbed her straw hat, too, and ran into Mama's room to say good-bye to her. She leaped out the door and jumped into the wagon. Mirah had forgotten the lunch basket, so she ran back to the porch and grabbed it from the table. She caught up with the wagon just as it was pulling out of the yard.

As they rode toward the other field, the girls sat on the tailgate and let their limber body rock up and down and from side to side. They raised their legs as high as they could to keep them from getting lashed and banged by the stinging weeds bent underneath the wagon as it rolled along the path. When they were not raising their legs out of the way of the weeds, they let them dangle and sway at will to each bump and grind in the path. Only once did Papa stop, and that was to let Mirah lower the pail of water into the spring in the creek to keep it cool for lunch.

Van sat in the buckboard with Papa. Ed braced himself on the side board, and begged Papa all the way to the field to let him hold the reins and drive the mules back home. Papa would not give in to Ed without a lecture about how to steer the mules, but that did not keep Ed from asking if he could drive them back home. After begging for several minutes, Ed finally coaxed Papa into saying yes. When Ed heard Papa's answer, he jumped up and down in the wagon and laughed for several minutes.

The wagon ride to the field each morning was no longer than half an hour, but to the girls it felt like only five minutes had passed before those long cotton rows they had to chop unfurled before their weary eyes. The drudgery of having to chop all those rows of cotton, and peanuts, too, when they were ready, was enough to make them sick and tired just looking at rows.

Mirah was first to put on her straw hat, pick up her hoe, and dig into the first clump of wire grass.

The hoe was so dull it wouldn't even cut grass. She called Papa to sharpen her hoe, and the others, too, with the file loaded into the wagon. Greta searched in the wagon for her big, long-sleeved shirt to help shield her arms from the hot sun but discovered she had forgotten to pick it up off the table when she ran into Mama's room to say goodbye to her. She hated the hot sun beaming down on her arms, so she needed the long sleeved shirt to protect them. Greta shoved her wide-brimmed straw hat on the back of her head and jumped out of the wagon, balancing herself on her hoe. Looking up, she realized that Ginger and Ed had already picked up their hoes and started chopping cotton and Mirah had finished getting her hoe filed. Greta's row was now behind theirs; she would be last to take a drink of water before she began a new row.

Greta didn't like chopping at all. It was dreadful walking up and down those long rows chopping and banging at tough wire grass that, most of the time, the hoe was too dull to cut. Wire grass had a mind of its own; it always appeared clean and shaven above the surface. Its roots, which are the biggest part of the hoeing, remained hidden underneath the soil until it rained. Although Greta tried as hard as she could, she always got scolded because of the grass she was leaving underneath the surface and between the tender plants. Being careful to chop a clean row, now her row was a long ways behind Ginger, Ed, and Mirah's. Even her sister Nita, only a small child, whenever she tried to chop cotton could keep up with Greta and chop almost as fast as she could.

The hot sun steadily beamed down on Greta's head mercilessly, and the harder she chopped the faster her head pounded. Her heart grew fainter by the minute and caused her to slow her pace even more. Her long, lanky legs basked more fully in the sun, and blistered her black, leathery skin. But she crept on, trying hard to chop a clean row so Mama would be proud and say nice things to her when she returned home. Greta's heart swelled with pride whenever Mama gloated over her.

The noon hour couldn't arrive fast enough for Greta, and she could tell by the shadow of the sun when it was time to quit for lunch. The sun now had perched itself directly over her head, enveloping the entire length of the shadow that outlined her frail body. She could see that Mirah and Ginger had already found a shady, cool spot to rest and were waiting for Greta to reach the end of her row before Ginger opened the lunch basket. Before they ate, though, Mirah walked to the creek to fetch the pail of water lowered into the spring

Papa and Van finally stopped the mules for lunch, unhitched them from the plows, and trekked up to the wagon, which had been parked in the shade underneath a tree.

Plowing and chopping the long rows at the back gate field was both dreadful and fun. The fun was riding in the wagon and using half an hour of just riding before getting to and from the field. Then they got one full hour at noontime to rest in the shade and eat lunch from the straw basket. There were no dishes to wash and put away and no minor chores to be done.

Ginger carefully removed the white cloth spread over the lunch basket and laid it aside. Then she opened the container of cabbage, fatback, and potatoes. She dipped up cabbage and potatoes and laid a biscuit and the biggest piece of fatback on Papa's plate. After Van and Ed had filled their plates, the girls took turns to pile their tin plates high with their lunch and sat down under the shade tree to eat. Papa, Ed, and Van ate their lunch in the wagon because they didn't want the ants on the ground crawling all over it.

Sometimes when they were chopping a field of cotton or peanuts away from the house, the girls rested in the middle portion of the wagon, usually on guano sacks filled with cotton and shaped like oversized pillows. Today, the wagon was partly exposed to the hot sun, so Greta just spread a pallet on the ground under a shade tree. The minute she did, Ginger and Mirah plopped down and stretched out on the flat of their backs before she could lie down herself. They rested quietly, eyes wide open, watching the huge oak leaves dance in the summer breeze above their heads. Often they played quiet games with strings or just stretched out on the pallet and dreamed of faraway places where there were no cotton rows to chop.

If it rained while they were at the field, the girls would fasten one end of a shabby tarp to a tree trunk and the other end to the wagon. They piled underneath the shelter and waited calmly for the shower to pass over. The showers were common on hot days; especially Papa and Van welcomed them because they cooled the earth they were plowing and gave them a much longer time to rest.

On other days when the chopping was light and easy, and the cotton was not so grassy, the girls took off during the noon hour to canvass the hedges along the edge of the field and load their hats with wild plums, mulberries, and blackberries. Other times they put them in the empty water pail and dropped it in the creek spring until it was time for them to go home. These berries were ripe and sweet; after the frost fell on them, they were sweeter and juicier as well. At the end of the day, while riding home from the field, these delicious wild fruits were a welcomed treat.

The spring water from the creek was a life saver for those who had to work at the back gate field because cool water was always available for their thirsty mouths and for keeping their berries cool. The creek, itself, was fascinating; and each time one of the girls walked across the rickety bridge to the other side, she stared long and hard into the creek to make a wish. The brown trout swished in the creek and the slick eels, too. They cooled themselves in the spring water, yet they were mindful of keeping their flickering eyes and mouths wide open to catch insects that might flutter nearby. None of the girls ever thought about catching any of this fish to eat. If they did catch them, they would become pets; besides, there was no time for pets and chopping, too. Now and then a water moccasin slithered by, moving steadily with the swiftly running creek water. The girls were afraid of snakes; and when they saw one, they jumped back from the edge of the creek until it swam out of sight.

After Papa and the boys had crammed their stomachs full of potatoes, meat, and cabbage and swallowed a gallon of water, Van lit up a cigarette and Papa smoked his pipe, sending up a long, streaming cloud of smoke that the girls watched until it faded into midair. When Ginger and Greta got tired of lying down, they sat up and rested their backs against the tree trunk. Usually Mirah took a nap under a shade tree after eating her lunch, but today, she picked blackberries along the edge of the field and lowered them into the creek to chill. The girls strained their ears to hear Papa and the Van talking in muffled tones about how the plowing was shaping up. They supposed that all this work wouldn't bring a good harvest in October if the weather didn't hold up.

Before the noon hour was up, Papa and the boys took turns taking short walks in the bushes to comfort themselves, but they were careful that the girls were not watching them. It seemed Papa never did sleep. Before Van drifted off to dream-land, he watched Papa squint-eyed when he pulled his watch from his shabby overalls and yelled, "It's time to get back to work!" When he spoke, they all jumped straight up on their feet; if they didn't, Papa came after them with a tree limb, threatening their lives. If they didn't move fast enough, he raised the tree limb high above their heads, ready to strike down on the workers at any moment. Papa used this same tree limb to stir Lucy and Ginny to let them know, too, that it was time to get back to work. The boys laughed to themselves when they found out that Papa was only using a trick to scare them and wouldn't dare hit them with a big tree limb.

The afternoon hours flew by quickly. The shad-ows grew longer, signaling the girls that the time was nearing when they will board the wagon and head home for a bumpy ride. Each girl and Ed chopped ten rows during the morning and after-noon; multiplying that number among the four of them, chopping would produce a whopping forty rows that day out of the 240 rows of cotton that needed chopping.

Greta looked up to see that Ginger, Ed, and Mirah had finished chopping their rows and were starting to meet hers. Greta chopped as fast as she could so they all could finish quickly. When they caught up Greta's row, she fell into Ginger's arms, thankful for the help she got, since her row was always behind everyone else's.

Papa and Van, who were plowing the peanut field, noticed the girls and Ed had chopped ten rows of cotton each, so they, too, started thinking about quitting for the evening. They thought about it alright, but they must have plowed a full thirty minutes more before finally stopping to hitch the mules to the wagon. While they were waiting for Papa and Van to stop plowing, Ginger, Greta, and Ed chopped one more row. They took turns to chop by sections in the row and left gaps for each other to chop until the one row was finished. Mirah left to fetch the pail with a few wild blackberries she picked at noon and dropped into the spring to cool.

Before they reach home, the girls will have eaten all the blackberries Mirah picked.

There never was free time. Farming was a way of life wherein everyone shared the work load. On days when chopping a field of cotton was nearly finished before the noon hour, Mama and the girls went to the field to chop, even Nita and Gaye, who took to playing in the sand at the end of the rows in the shade.

The afternoon was spent resting and doing a few field chores: The flower beds and gardens were chopped and fertilized; Vegetables were gathered, cooked, and eaten at mealtime; and blackberries were picked at the back gate and made into a delicious cobbler.

On days when Papa and Van finished a field of plowing before the chopping was done, it was hard to coax them into plowing the garden or weeding the long rows of sweet potatoes. With a lot of begging and pleading, this job was always given to Ed, who rarely did a good job. The plowing that no one else wanted to do was gladly put upon his shoulders. Ed was ridiculed and cajoled about the sloppy way he plowed the crops. No one thought he could plow the garden well, so he didn't even try; he just did what he was told to do.

When it was finally time to stop plowing, Papa and Van hitched Lucy and Ginny to the wagon and headed home. Van was frightened every minute while Ed was driving the wagon homeward, as Papa had promised him he could do. Ed's mind told him not to go straight home from the field like Papa though he would; today, he went a different way on a path that wound around the field past some old, rotting houses. Something was eerie about these old shacks that Ed loved looking at; he was drawn to them and gazed at each one until they were out of sight. Some of those old houses were empty and rundown. Others still had families living in them who did not own the houses. Squatters and gypsies, the country folks called them. They didn't attend church and visited no one. They were a seedy lot who wandered from one farm to another gleaning the fields of peanuts and cotton. They picked wild plums, chinquapin nuts, muscadines, and fox grapes among the groves at the end of the rows. They made a living out of borrowing from other folks and had no intentions of paying them back. What little they begged had to last them until they begged for more.

No one knew for sure why Ed took the wagon by these old rundown shacks. But Ed drove on, waving at the scraggly children who ran out to the end of the path just to see who was passing by and to beg for a piece of bread and meat. Seeing how hungry these children were, Ed stopped the wagon long enough for Greta to throw them a biscuit left-over from the lunch. The tallest child caught it in her hands and ran back to the house to tell her mama that the woman in the wagon gave her something to eat. Trying to hide her full view in the doorway, a woman stuck her head outside the door and looked around. No sooner had she closed the door than she began to scold the child. Greta sighed as she watched the shadow of the woman's arm raise and lash out at the hungry child.

Papa's family had lived and died in the next old empty house, but he moved out when he was a young boy. Going by the house today and gazing into the huge front yard brought back his boyhood memories. He thought about his slave parents, cousins, sisters, and brothers who had grown up, married, and long ago passed away; others lived on farms away from the area. Papa didn't believe the rumors flying around the countryside about ghosts dwelling in his family's old house. How could his parents and cousins still live in that old run-down farmhouse? He never failed to look through the gaping front door, hoping to detect any sign of recall about his childhood, of later life, or any little movement in these shacks. And sure enough, this time when he gazed with empty eyes, he thought he saw the figures of his mammy and pappy gaz-ing back at him. He strained his eyes trying to see through the front door that had long ago fallen off the hinges. Half frightened and half anxious, Papa's eyes got glued on the image he saw of his mammy and pappy in the old house staring back at him. He jumped up from the buckboard in the wagon, yelled "halt!" to the mules, and leaped from the wagon in pursuit of what he had just seen. Lucy and Ginny bucked, neighed loudly, and started to run just as Van snatched the reins from Ed's hands and settled them down. They reared and stomped the ground, but Van kept his strong grip on them. The girls in the wagon started to cry in fear, but Papa kept running toward the old house.

"Come back here, Papa!" Greta Complained. "This old house got hants in 'em. Somebody's trying to scare us and I don't want us to drive by heah anymore!" Seeing how Greta was too frightened to move, Papa just stepped up his pace and ran head-on toward the old shack where he had seen the ghosts of his mammy and pappy. With his two hands cupped to the transom window, he stared through the empty rooms into the back yard. He saw that the frame in just one of the rooms had been attacked by cobwebs that partly sealed the room where he once slept. He let his eyes rove around and stop at the gnarled, dead oak tree in the back yard. Standing there looking through the transom window, he gazed in shocking disbelief at what he saw.

Staring harder and letting his eyes travel slowly upward to the tree top, he saw some ropes and ragged clothes that still clung to a man's Skelton. The skull's eyes had rotted, leaving sockets where the eyes once were. One of the arms had fallen from its joint and dropped to the ground below the skeleton. One thigh still attached to the skeleton had nearly rotted down to the knee and sagged underneath its shredded britches, waiting for the maggots to eat away at the last bit of dried, crusty flesh. The shackles the man wore clutched the ankle and clumped on the ground below the skeleton. Without saying a word, Papa wondered about the man who was hung there, but he never found out why he disappeared and lived alone in this old deserted shack. The people who lived around there rumored that the man had been lynched, but Papa couldn't believe it. The whole neighborhood had no idea where Mr. Roach had disappeared.

Today, Papa knew the answer and was too frightened to tell anyone.

The sweat trickled down Papa's face in round beads as he hastily climbed back into the wagon. His hair was wet and slick—so were his clothes. He wondered what he had done that made his mammy and pappy want to scare him so, especially since they had all died many, many years ago. He thought they all loved him, but after today's horror, he was so frightened that what he had seen was unspeakable.

Van would not let Ed have the reins to drive further down the path. Noticing how Papa was too shaken to drive, and having seen such a haunting sight, Papa was more determined that the wagon went straight home and was not concerned about who drove. Neither did anyone admit to Papa what they thought he had just seen.

Van led the mules homeward, struggling to keep them on the narrow path. There was an old, narrow, rickety bridge to cross further down the path, and he hoped the wagon wheel would not get stuck in the rotten holes where the boards had been patched over many times. The poles and planks had nearly broken from the weight of the mules and wagon trotting over them.

Steering the mules calmly, Van started them pulling in a slow trot a-ways back so they could gather enough speed to sail across the bridge without catching a wheel in the holes that could land the wagon in the ditch. By the time the wagon reached the gaping holes, Van made sure the mules were galloping at full speed. Over the bumpy logs they trotted in a mad dash to reach the other side of the bank. Clearing it with a snap, the plows, lunch basket, and hoes banged and clattered, and then leaped and bounced all over the wagon. When the wagon slowed down, all its contents and everyone in it had shifted. No one was sitting in the buckboard, and the girls were strewn among the plows and hoes. Ginger let out a screeching howl when the huge plow blade lurched up and sliced wide open a long gash in the side of her leg, splattering blood all over her clothes and leaving a big round puddle in the wagon. Grabbing her ankle, pain from the gash shot up her leg and sent her into scream-ing hysterics. She flung off her shirt, bandaged the wound, and held it tightly with her trembling hand until the bleeding stopped. On Van drove, though, toward the back gate as if nothing had happened.

No one in the wagon was anxious to pass the old graveyard site where all their aunts, uncles, babies, grand pappy and grand mammy, sisters, brothers, and other distant ancestors were bur-ied. Many times Mama had carried the girls to these unkempt graves to clean the wire grass and weeds from them. On these trips, they cleaned the tombstones, making sure that each name could be clearly read from a distance. Then Mama went over each name of the ancestors and told a short tale about each one. The graves that had been there the longest were beginning to sink and were in much need of being filled up with dirt again. From the looks of them today, no one had been to the back gate to care for these graves in years.

Papa had told them many stories about grave-yards, too, and today, he was quick to remind the girls that when graves sink, spirits of the person in the grave return to haunt them. Gazing deeply into the sunken holes around the graves as they drove by them, Mirah's eyes got attached to her grand mammy and grand pappy's graves. She could see a glimpse of what appeared to be the corner of a pine box with its lid partly open. Horrified at what she saw in the graves, she wondered if her grand mammy and grand pappy had, indeed, escaped from their graves to the old shack they just passed. She knew without a doubt that they had gone to the old rundown shack, but she wouldn't dare ask the question. She was just too frightened to think about it and didn't even want to know what the answer might be. Mirah was shattered when she thought that what Papa had just seen through the window in the old house was actually a ghost.

"Whoa!" yelled Van, as he headed the mules toward the house and over a steep hill. They were picking up speed now, so he yelled again, "Whoa!"

He tried to take the mules slowly downhill. Going downhill in the wagon shoved all the farm equipment and passengers toward the front end of the wagon, so everything was in an uproar again. The girls will have to climb into the front of the wagon, rake all the contents to the back, and unload everything from the tailgate. Indeed, that was a task they hated to do. Once they were home, they just wanted to unload their junk and get off the wagon.

When they reached the shade of the old cottonwood tree in the back yard, Mirah and Greta jumped out the wagon first, holding on to each other to keep from falling. Then Mirah helped Ginger climb down from the wagon while she held the rag on the gash in her leg. By now her face was frowning from the pain that sent her toward the porch hopping on one foot. Greta picked up the lunch basket, shirts, and straw hats and walked toward the house. Then the boys jumped out of the wagon and began emptying its entire contents on the ground.

Papa could barely steady his hands to unhitch the mules, yet he had told the boys many times not to be afraid of ghosts. Now, Papa had frightened the girls when he got scared; he was not as tough as they thought he was. After Van saw that Papa was unstable, he rushed over to lead Lucy and Ginny toward the barn. Then he and Ed drew a trough of water for the mules to drink and tossed them a bundle of fodder and oats from the barn to eat. They left the mules starting to eat and to rest while Van and Ed headed across the yard and into the house. Papa sat down quietly on the porch, thinking to himself about what had happened to him.

At fifteen years old, Lola was taking care of the house for Mama. After the wagon carrying the field workers had left the yard early and headed past the barn over to the back gate field across the creek to work, Lola went into the kitchen to wash up the breakfast dishes. Today, she was left behind to care for Mama and the baby, wash clothes for the family, mind the younger girls, Nita and Gay, and cook supper for the family. Her hands were full, yet she hated doing all that housework. Lola was glad she wasn't working in the field today because the hot sun scalds her fair skin and leaves it swollen and puffy.

If the clothes had not been washed when the girls returned from the field, they were told to help Lola finish washing them as well as helping with other tasks she was left to do around the house. The field workers really didn't like doing this; they felt that if one of them had stayed at home, all the work would be done. Like that, the girls could enjoy a few hours for private time in the evening.

As soon as Lola had finished the breakfast dishes, Mama called her to help bathe the baby. First she set a kettle of water on the back of the stove to get hot so Mama could use warm water to bathe little Brownese. Then she found a soft clean bathing cloth and castile soap for the baby's bath. It seemed as though Brownese had already gained two or three ounces. Her tiny hands waved more aimlessly now, and her beautiful brown eyes followed Lola wherever she went in the room.

This morning, Mama got out of bed for the first time since the baby arrived. Lola helped her to stand steadily on her feet and make her way to the soft-cushioned rocking chair beside the bed. Lola set the pan of warm water near the chair and put the soap and cloth in the pan. Then she spread a bath drying cloth in Mama's lap. Smiling, Lola laid Brownese in Mama's arms and gloated over the chance to pick the baby up and play with her. As soon as the bathing was over, Mama put a cloth diaper and handmade nightshirt on Brownese and nursed her. Halfway through the nursing, Brownese closed her eyes and drifted off to sleep. Lola placed her in the crib beside Mama's bed and left the room to prepare Mama's breakfast of toasted biscuits, bacon, and oatmeal. Then Lola sat down to eat her own breakfast before getting the washtubs ready to begin scrubbing the clothes.

Lola set two galvanized washtubs on a bench sitting on the back porch and put a washing board in the one where she would be scrubbing the clothes. Next, she pumped several gallon buckets of cold water from the well, poured them into the rinsing tub, and filled it to the brim. Then she dumped a half bottle of bluing in the water. She went to the pantry to get a large cake of lye soap that she placed in the wash basin on the bench. Finally, she lifted the kettle of boiling water off the stove and poured a bit of it over the lye soap to let it soften. Lola refilled the kettle with cold water and set it back on the stovetop to get boiling hot again for scalding the baby's clothes.

After the water had reached a boiling hot temperature in the wash pot on the woodpile, Lola toted three or four buckets to the washtub on the porch where the clothes would be washed. This round, black pot was also used to boil the dingy white clothes to make them sparkling clean and glistening white, but Lola had made up her mind that she wouldn't be doing that today.

A bucket of cold water was drawn from the well to mix with the hot water. Lola filled the tub with the white clothes and began scrubbing them vigorously, stopping now and then to smear the melting lye soap over each piece, and scrubbing it again. After inspecting each garment to see if she had cleaned it, Lola dumped it into the washtub holding the bluing rinse water. They lay there to soak until she finished washing all the white-and-light colored clothes.

These clothes will be rinsed and hung on the line with clothespins and then hoisted high enough so the morning fresh air could dry them before she started washing the colored and dark clothes. Lola repeated this process, using the same bluing rinse water. Before the dark clothes were ready to be hung on the line, she took off the white-and-light colored ones that were dry to make space on the clothesline for the darker ones.

Just as Lola had hung the last load of colored clothes on the line and hoisted the pole as high as she could get it, she noticed a muddy, rickety-looking black car coming straight down the path toward the house. "Who could be coming for a visit this early in the afternoon?" She wondered. Lola grabbed Nita and Gaye's hand and cautioned them to stop playing in the yard. "Shoo," she warned, and led them inside the house and sent them upstairs to their room to hide and stay hid until the car leaves. She had seen Mama do this many times, so Lola felt that they would be safe upstairs and that she, herself, could handle the folks in the car.

Lola stretched her neck to see who it was as the jalopy crept closer and closer to the house. The car pulled up to an abrupt halt in the yard, jerking before it finally stopped. Lola walked briskly up to the car. Snarling, she asked, "What y'all want?" Peering deeper into the car, she saw that a skinny, slight man was driving two fat women who had barely wedged themselves inside a one-seat car that was not wide enough to hold a skinny man and two fat women. "A band of gypsy thieves," Lola thought. "I'll have problems with them."

"Do you have anything you would like to get rid of today?" one of the fat gypsy hags asked.

Lola looked her straight in the eyes and said, "No!"

"Well, we could use eggs, old clocks, and picture frames," the other woman insisted. "We also can give you twenty-five cents for picture frames, and fifty cents for old clocks."

"No, thank you," Lola replied again, politely. She hoped the gypsies would leave the yard and go on about their business. But that did not happen; they did not leave the yard as she thought they would.

Lola tried to reason with the gypsies and explain to them that she was busy with the washing, cooking, and helping her mama with her new baby. Mama had warned the girls about the power of gypsy bands who rove around the countryside trying to gyp anyone out of what little items their families owned. It seemed to Lola that these gypsies didn't want to hear what she was saying. The little man got out of the car and started walking about in the yard. His eyes targeted everything within their scope and left Lola to argue with the gypsy hags in the car.

Lola could see the man making his way to the steps, so she ran toward the porch and jumped in front of him and begged him not to go into her house. Mama called out from the room to ask Lola who she was talking to. Hearing this, Lola stepped inside the screen door onto the porch to answer Mama. Within a minute, one of the gypsy hags had gotten out of the car and followed the man to the door. The minute Lola stepped inside, the gypsy hag grabbed the door and held it open until she and the skinny little man forced their way inside and pushed past Lola into the room where Mama sat beside her new baby. Seeing this infant child, the gypsy hag's eyes lit up. She got nosey and started asking how many children Mama had. Continuing to admire the baby and fuss over her beautiful, bronze curly hair and light brown skin, Lola could tell right away that she wanted to take the child from Mama.

Spine-tingling fear struck Mama and Lola when they looked at each other. Lola thought about Papa and the girls, plowing and chopping the field on the other side of the creek and that they were too far away from the house to hear her scream for help.

Mama knew she couldn't show any signs of fear, or else the gypsy hag would take the child and run back to the car. Lola thought she knew how to defend herself, but she couldn't help seeing that the gypsy hag's attention was stuck on Brownese lying helplessly in the cradle. She inched closer and closer toward the cradle and leaned over to stare at Brownese. She stood ready to grab the baby the minute Mama's attention was distracted.

Lola's thoughts quickly settled on how she could get these gypsies out of her house without panicking. She eased out of Mama's room, tip-toed toward the cook stove, and whispered to Nita and Gaye, "Get back upstairs." Lola grabbed the kettle of boiling hot water off the stove that was needed to scald the baby's clothes. Holding the kettle behind her skirt, she slowly moved toward the gypsy hag. With all the strength she had in her body, she sloshed the kettle of hot water toward the gypsy hag's head and scalded her across the ear, neck, face, and arm, barely missing Brownese's head as she lay tummy down in her crib.

Flying past Lola toward the door, the gypsy hag held her scalded face in her hands as she screamed and cursed in pain. The hot water scaled the little man's arm, but he was too frightened to speak, so both of them broke out of the room at the same time and jumped from the porch into the yard. Stumbling with leaps and bounds, they tore open the car doors. The skinny man and the fat gypsy hag piled into the front seat on top of the other fat hag sitting there in a daze, half whimpering and screaming, wondering what had happened. Just as Lola ran into the yard with the kettle to pitch another dose of hot water on the gypsies, the man started up the car. With a roar and sputter, he whirled it around, spun from the yard, and sped down the pathway toward the road. Lola watched in fear that they might return as the car turned out of the pathway, leaving a trail of dust behind as it drove down the road. These gypsies might pester other families today, but Lola was sure they would never wander into her yard again.

"Are you okay, Mama?" Lola asked. Mama's eyes lit up with wonder.

"Yes," Mama answered. She told Lola that gypsies can smell a newly born baby because they always come snooping around. And how they know this is a mystery. Worse still, they can make their trinkets appear far more important than your own children. Lola had heard of these encounters with roving gypsy thieves before, but she never thought it would ever happen to her family. Today, she became braver and more quick-witted than she thought she ever could be, but the fear of those gypsies remained with her for the rest of her days.

Lola had used up her lunch time with these good-for-nothing gypsy thieves, so now it was time to start cooking supper. She could eat later, so she managed to fix Mama a bowl of white potato soup and a biscuit that was leftover from breakfast. Nita and Gaye were hungry, too, and Lola tried not to notice them hiding behind the door. "You can go outside and play now," she said, handing each of them a biscuit spread with blackberry jelly. "The gypsies wanted to steal our baby sister, but I scared them away," bragged Lola.

"I'll kill them if they come back here!" Nita said.

"Me, too, won't I, Lola?" Gaye added.

Lola could imagine a shocked and surprised look on Papa's face if she told him how she had battled with gypsies. She didn't want the story seem scarier than what it had been, so she made up her mind not to tell Papa about the incident and just mention that some visitors came by. If she had told, Papa would demand that Lola, Mama, and the baby go to the field with him for fear that someone came while he was away and stole their belongings. Lola wanted Mama to get stronger before going to the field, so she wouldn't be telling Papa anything that happened that day.

Lola knew of cases when women go to work in the field within a couple of days after a baby is born, but she didn't want Mama doing that. She vowed to stay with Mama and to secure her as well as possible. At least a few weeks longer couldn't hurt until Mama could get around much better. Then she could get her own meals and look after herself.

When the family sat down to eat, Lola did not want to make a big to-do over what happened today. All secrets, those with Papa's encounter with the ghosts and Lola's struggle with the gypsies, were kept for quiet corners. Such stories would scare the younger girls and should not be discussed openly. No matter how painful, those who were involved tucked their heads and never said a single word about the incidents they had that day. They would be discussed between Mama and Papa away from the listening ears of the girls.

During summertime and on rainy days, when the fieldwork was at a standstill, all the girls knew what that meant. There were clothes to mend and closets, bedrooms, pantry, and dresser drawers to be emptied, cleaned, and their contents rearranged. Floors needed scrubbing and waxing, and the parlor dusted. The girls had repeated these tasks so many times that they knew exactly what needed to be done, but when the rain kept up for a couple of days, there was more cleaning time and clothes to mend than ever before. Usually Lola, Mirah, Greta, and Ginger were told to do these jobs, and they seemed to always do them well. Nita and Gaye were becoming big girls now, and they soon would be passing on some of the work to them.

The girls knew Mama would be supervising the cleaning and mending clothes because she was getting out of bed for a few hours a day. When she felt stronger, she would be up all day, and help with the housework as well. Mama put everything under close inspection and examined every crevice and corner to make sure the girls dusted and cleaned thoroughly all the dirt from the house. She couldn't trust the girls to go for long periods of time without checking their rooms. Sometimes they forgot to make up their beds or sweep under them every day, but the girls did not know when Mama would make her rounds inspecting their rooms. Whenever she did, there was always something that needed to be cleaned again. This kept up all summer long during rainy days.

Mama singled out dresser drawers that hadn't been emptied, closets to be rearranged, and clothes to be folded neatly in the drawers. Shoes were to be placed in cardboard boxes and never should be left strewn over the floor. If Mama found any misplaced shoes, she hid one of them; when the girls looked for the missing shoe, it was nowhere to be found. Mama didn't mind yelling either, especially when she caught the girls sitting idly about in their rooms, wasting away daylight hours—so she called it.

Mending the clothes was Lola and Mirah's job. Mama had taught Lola how to sew on the new Singer treadle machine she bought on time from the door-to-door salesman last winter. Mama searched the closets and dresser drawers looking for all the torn and ripped dresses and slips for the girls that needed mending. She stacked them neatly in a pile on the floor beside the machine. No sooner had she finished gathering them than Mirah found other clothes that Mama had overlooked for mending. Lola hated for Mirah to do this, so she begged her to stop looking for more clothes to mend. She asked her to sew on missing buttons and patch a few of the clothes Mama laid near the machine with the needle and thread.

Lola wished many times that she could make that treadle machine hum when it sews like Mama could. The few lessons she learned in her high school class did not measure up to how well Mama could sew. Mama could make the fancy dresses she saw in the Sears catalogue, but Lola knew that Mama could not afford to buy piece goods. Lola was the one who got most of the new clothes, and the other girls wore hand-me-downs. With six girls and a baby girl, the clothes had nearly worn out before the younger girls could fit in them. The clothes worn by Lola and Mirah were handed down to Ginger and Greta. Nita's clothes that had gotten too small for her were passed on to Gaye. Mama had already sewn baby clothes for Brownese, but as soon as she was able to, she would sew Brownese some toddler dresses.

It was difficult for Lola to get that treadle machine to sew. After she thought she had carried the thread through all the loops and bends correctly, she had a hard time getting the needle threaded. Using lamplight during the daytime to help Lola see well enough to thread the needle was no help at all, but she didn't give up. After getting the needle threaded, it started to sew right, else the thread jerked out of the needle again. When that happened, she couldn't tell if it was the bobbin that was threaded wrong or if she missed a step carrying the thread through all the loops in the upper part of the machine.

Lola finally got the machine needle threaded and was just beginning to stitch for three or four minutes when the thread knotted up underneath the cloth again and refused to sew. She summoned Mama at the top of her voice to help. Mama never got angry or yelled at Lola for not remembering what to do when she had a problem with the sewing machine, but Lola just ran out of patience this time.

Mama was at her side instantly. She pushed Lola from the chair in front of the machine and sat down to show Lola once more how to thread it. "Look at what I'm doing, Lola," she said, with her kind, patient voice. Mama carried the thread slowly through a maze of loops and hinges. "The thread must go this way around the top loop first, and then through the bottom loop," she told Lola. Then Mama checked the bobbin; it seemed to work okay. "Try it again," Mama added. "It should work well now." Mama got up from the chair and moved back to watch Lola start stitching again. Hearing the machine humming, Mama left Lola to do the mending and strained her neck to see what Mirah was doing. Mama tugged Papa's shirt from Mirah's hands and told her that she needed to take those buttons off that she had sewn on the shirt.

"Take them off?" Mirah asked angrily. "What for, Mama?"

"You will have to match each button with the ones on the shirt," Mama told her. "If there are no matching buttons in the sewing box, leave the shirt alone; I will buy shirt buttons when I go to town Saturday."

"Okay, Mama, I did all this sewing for nothing." Mirah snapped. She rolled her eyes at Mama and snatched the shirt from her hands.

Lola had the sewing machine whirring now as though she had perfected its operation. Picking up one garment after another to mend and placing each one under the needle on the feeder plate, her nimble fingers guided each rip and tear along the seams. "O-o-ouch!" Lola screamed, catching her breath. "Mama, Mama, I stuck the needle through my finger nail," Lola screamed again. "The needle went through my fingernail, Mama, and it broke off and splattered blood all over Nita's blouse I was mending." Lola cried. Dashing breathlessly to Lola's side, Mama gazed down in awe at what this child had done. Mama told Lola that the broken part of the needle would have to be removed from her fingernail.

"Don't move!" Mama shouted at Lola. "Stay where you are until I burn the tip of a needle to sterilize it before I pick for the broken needle lodged underneath your finger nail."

Lola hated the attention she was getting from her sisters because she knew Mama was determined to jab her finger until she removed that broken needle stuck underneath her nail. She was already scared and hurting from the puncture wound, and now Mama would have to probe her nail more deeply to remove the tip of the needle.

"Steady your hand," Mama kept saying, but Lola was so scared she couldn't stop trembling. "Mirah, look for some cotton, a clean cloth, and fetch me a pan of warm water, too," Mama demanded. Mama followed Mirah into the hallway and told her to hurry up.

Mama kept up the picking and squishing Lola's fingernail for what seemed like a whole hour. Finally she could see the tip of the silver needle peeking through the tiny hole in Lola's fingernail. Each time Mama pressed on her finger, blood oozed out and exposed the silvery tip hidden beneath the nail. As soon as she stopped pressing, the tip of the needle hid underneath the nail again. This was a stubborn needle tip to remove from Lola's finger, so Mama reluctantly gave up trying to get the needle to escape. Mama insisted that the needle will have to stay there until infection sets in. Then, if she presses on the nail, the needle will pop out and let the wound heal quickly. Stepping up the crying, Lola's mending job was ended in pain.

For nearly a whole week, Lola kept that wounded finger all bandaged up to her wrist. On the fifth day, she opened the bandage and gazed down at her finger and saw that the tip of the needle had forced itself through the same hole that encrusted it. Reaching down with her forefinger and thumb nails clutched together, Lola pulled the needle tip out of her finger. What followed was blood and pus flooding the punctured wound. "Look, Mama!" Lola exclaimed. "Here's the needle tip that broke off in my finger."

"Throw it away, child!" Mama asserted with disgust.

Over the next few days, Lola forgot about the terrible accident with the sewing machine. She went about her housework, but she was leery about using the sewing machine from that day on. She promised herself to always be careful whenever she was told to mend her sisters' dresses.

Ginger and Greta didn't mind keeping the kitchen, dining room, and parlor clean and looking pretty. The pantry in the kitchen was one of the main areas that needed cleaning. Ginger and Greta removed all the pots and pans and made sure each one was hung in its proper place. On one end of the shelf were pot lids that had been scattered and placed in no particular order. These were reassembled and stacked according to size.

They removed all the canned goods from the shelf and wiped the dust from underneath each jar Mama had placed there. The tops of the jars of butter beans, tomatoes, corn, and field peas were dusted. The jars of fruit containing pears, blackberries, and peaches that had been canned recently were dusted as well. When they finished dusting them, they were placed back on the shelf in neat order.

Greta opened the cook stove oven door and saw that the oven was covered with burned black spots left from the meals baked. Stretching her neck inside the oven, she knew lye soap was the only thing that could remove the stubborn spots. She took a bar of the soap and a rag and began to scrub the ugly spots very hard. The black baked spots would not come off, so she rubbed more lye soap on them and let it set to eat away the burned grease. The eyes on top of the stove where fatback, fish, and chicken were fried and where pots boiled over also were black and greasy. Greta found that these black sticky spots had made stubborn stains, but she scrubbed and scrubbed them until they were clean. When she finished cleaning the stovetop, Greta found a rag and pumped a bucket of water from the well. She got down on her hands and knees to scrub and wax the kitchen floor.

After Greta finished, she went into the dining room to help Ginger dust the china closet shelves where all of Mama's best dishes were kept in neat order. Ginger handed Greta each piece carefully as she removed it from the shelf because these dishes were Mama's Sunday best that she used to serve meals to her company. There was a pink glass dinner set Mama collected when Lola and Mirah sold candy for their sixth and seventh grade classes. An old tall Chinese teapot, with cups and saucers to match, were so special that Mama set all of them on a separate shelf. Lots and lots of mismatched water glasses were on the next shelf that had been won at carnivals or purchased from the five-and-dime store. No one dared to go into the china closet without asking Mama's permission. She was so afraid that the girls would break one of her good glasses, and no one would know who did it. Not that it mattered that much, but the girls were not careful with her things. Ginger wiped the shelves clean underneath the dinner plates and made sure that each piece was handled carefully and placed back on the shelves just as she had found them. Ginger swept the dining room floor and Greta mopped it clean. After the linoleum dried, she gave it a shine that would glisten in the dark.

Ginger and Greta began cleaning the parlor next. Of all the rooms in the house, this one was where Mama and Papa entertained special guests. The parlor was also Lola and Mirah's special courting room when boys came around or when Mama's lady friends visited. Ginger and Greta had fun cleaning this room, for it gave them a chance to reminisce about all the company they had seen come and go and the specialty items and old curios that were hidden there. An old grandfather clock sagged on the wall between the two front windows. In the corner next to it was a mahogany whatnot shelf where Mama placed all the tiny objects she had collected over the years. She kept Papa's gilded porcelain shaving mug there that she gave him for a wedding gift. No one knew its value, but just keeping it reminded Mama and Papa of days when they were young lovers and courting.

On the wall just above the rickety divan were family portraits. Mammy and Pappy's pictures and their families were hanging there. Papa's brothers, sisters, and their children took up half of the wall; on the other half of the wall were Mama's sisters, brothers, and their children. The oval and square lopsided frames held all the relatives, but on the wall across from the sofa, Mama and Papa's portraits of themselves were hung in identical oval ivory frames.

Mama's picture showed an elegant lady who appeared noble enough to be a queen. Her hair was pushed up in a thick roll across the top of her head. A big, wide black velvet bow caught up the hair at the back of her neck. Mama wore a prominent smile on her face that she pressed into a smirk at the corners of her mouth. She put on her best outfit for this picture: a white lace blouse with a stiff stand-up collar that clutched the bottom of her chin. Her chest stood out with pride as she captured this happy moment.

Papa was a gentle man, and he showed every bit of a dapper gentleman in his portrait. All the children loved Papa's boyish charm he showed on his round face. His hair, parted on the side, had been slicked down with Vaseline and brushed to one side, making wavy curls that flowed down the side of his head. Papa's neatly trimmed beard barely touched his mustache, which curled up at the corners of his mouth. His lips were thin and demanding when he opened them to speak, even with the slightest tone of voice. His black dapper suit lapel was graced with a white rose boutonniere that sprang from the buttonhole. His black vest practically enveloped a fancy white long-sleeved cuffed shirt that fastened up to the neck. Papa was as handsome as a doll, and his cool manner reflected each nice comment anyone made about him. As soon as guests entered the parlor, his portrait met their eyes and greeted them with "Welcome" and "Stay a while."

After fluffing and turning over the divan pillows, Ginger dusted the armrests. The coffee table and three-legged stool in the corner were also dusted and polished. Then Ginger mopped the linoleum in the parlor, being careful not to let water seep underneath the worn cracks. Again, Greta got down on her hands and knees to wax the parlor linoleum. She polished hard and long to make it shine, even though it had worn thin.

Lola and Mirah cleaned the spots from the oven that Greta had left to soak. They were anxious to start cooking supper on a sparkling clean oven and shiny stovetop eyes. After making a fire in the cook stove, cabbage was cooked in a steamer above a pot of water. In little or no time, the water came to a roiling boil on the round eye. Mirah sliced ham and put it in the black skillet to fry, sending out a lingering aroma that drew Papa and the boys toward the house craving for something to eat. Sliced sweet potatoes were fried and smothered in the skillet. The biscuits Lola baked in the hot oven were brown and crispy, and they waited for the family to eat them with their supper. A kettle of water steeped on back of the stove that would be used to wash the supper dishes. "Tonight, it will be pleasant in this house," Lola sighed.

III. BURIED HOPE

Lola and Mirah traveled back and forth to a segregated high school each day when they were not needed at home to help Mama. The school bus did not stop in front of the house to pick them up. They arose early in the morning and walked two miles through the woods to the highway to catch the bus. When they returned from school in the evenings, it was time to eat supper.

Early during the school year, Mama stopped sending Ginger and Greta to elementary school because they were not graduating; however, they begged and begged Mama to let them keep going. They were two crestfallen young girls who had missed a lot of time in school, but Mama was afraid to reveal their handicaps of not being able to hear well. Much worse, their hearing loss kept them from learning to read, write, and speak correctly. The teacher never understood what they were saying, and the school children picked on them because of it. Mama tried to shield them from ridicule, but the teacher never offered to help Ginger and Greta. No one ever asked why they were not going to school.

Van had long ago stopped going to elementary school. He barely made it through the sixth grade, and when Van did quit, he had learned nothing. Papa said he only knew how to plow the land and take in the harvest. During the winter months, Van wished for something to do until plowing time because he feared Papa would make him return to school. Ed, who never entered school, and Van who really didn't mind staying at home that much, kept themselves busy doing routine farm work. The weekends were left for visiting friends and hitching a quick run to town with anyone who would stop to give them a ride.

Mama promised the girls she would take them to the county fair in the fall. The girls had known since school let out in the spring that the fair was coming to town. School would be dismissing the students on a Friday so the bus could be used to transport them into town. Ginger and Greta had missed a lot of days from school, but Mama wanted them to have a big treat at the fair, too. She got permission from Nita and Gaye's teacher to take Ginger and Greta to the fair along with the other children on the school bus.

Mama spent the whole day before the fair getting the girls ready. First, she washed the dresses, underclothes, and socks for the girls to wear and hung them on the line to dry. Second, their patent leather shoes were polished with Vaseline, and their white ones were smeared with white shoe polish. After the socks dried, they were paired and tucked neatly into each child's shoes. When the dresses were nearly dry, Mama took them from the line and rolled them to dampen. After the dampness had spread throughout the dresses, she ironed each one with the two irons she set on the stovetop to get hot. When Mama had finished ironing the dresses, she matched each one with ribbons for the girls' hair and laid them on the sofa in the parlor room away from the busy eyes of the children. After Ginger and Greta killed two chicken fryers, plucked their feathers, and cut them up into frying parts, Mama fried the two chickens for herself and the girls' lunch at the fair. She set the chicken in the pantry for safe keeping. Ginger and Greta took their baths in the round galvanized washtub before the other girls got home from school; after their baths Ginger and Greta cooked supper for the family.

At the end of the school day, Nita and Gaye ran home and helped with the house chores. After they ate supper, Mama called Nita and Gaye to take their baths in the washtub she lugged upstairs. She let the girls fill the tub halfway with cold water from the pump. Next, she took a black kettle of scalding hot water upstairs and mixed it with the cold water so they could wash themselves in the tub together. Mama searched for wash rags for the girls to bathe with, and found an old worn-out sheet for a drying towel that they would use to dry themselves off. She used a cake of Ivory soap she hid in her room out of the girls' reach and flung it into the tub of warm water to make lather with the wash rag for the girls. She left the soap upstairs until all the girls had finished bathing.

Nita and Gaye got into the tub together and washed their arms, between their legs, scrubbed their feet, and washed their backsides. When they finished bathing, they dried themselves with the cloth, put on their underclothes, and went to bed. Before long, Nita and Gaye went to sleep while thinking about the fun they would have at the fair.

After Lola and Mirah returned from school, as soon as they put their books down, they ate supper. After they finished eating, they grabbed the tub of water that Nita and Gaye used to bathe in, carried it through the front door, set it on the ground, and dumped it. Then they took the tub to the pump out-side the kitchen door and half filled it up again with cold water. Another kettle of water on the stove had gotten hot enough to make a warm tub of water for Lola and Mirah to bathe in. After they had warmed the water suitably for a bath, they carried the tub of water upstairs and set it in the middle of the floor. Lola dipped half of the water out and filled up a large wash basin, which she used to bathe in; and Mirah sat down in the tub to take her bath. When they both finished, Lola poured her dirty water into the big tub, which they left to dump the next morn-ing. At last, they both jumped into bed.

Mama bathed Brownese and put her to bed. Within minutes, Brownese went to sleep. Then Mama washed and dusted herself with talcum powder and got into bed for a comfortable night's rest.

Papa awoke the girls bright and early the next morning, since he was not going to the fair. He hoped Van and Ed would catch a ride to the fair with some of the older boys. Besides, Mama told them if they were not in school, they were not allowed to ride the school bus. If they didn't get a ride, Papa promised to drive the wagon to town Saturday and take them to the fair.

Mirah came downstairs the next morning to start the breakfast of milk, oatmeal, biscuits, and pear preserves while Lola dressed herself and helped Nita and Gaye put on their shoes and socks. Ginger and Greta came downstairs, after they had dressed in their socks, shoes, and slips, and sat down at the table to eat a bowl of oatmeal.

Mama placed a bowl of oatmeal in front of Nita and Gaye; instantly they slurped it down. The chair was too low for Brownese to sit up to the table, so she sat on Mama's lap, grabbing and stuffing the buttered biscuit from Mama's plate into her mouth as fast as she could. Then Brownese raised the cup of milk to her tiny lips and drank it all up, spilling a little out the sides of her mouth. "Oatmeal," she said to Mama, and reached for the spoon in Mama's bowl.

Mama sat Brownese down while she gave Nita and Gaye their outfits they were wearing to the fair and sent them upstairs, where Ginger and Greta waited to help them get dressed. Mama slipped Brownese's pink dress on her and tied a pink bow around a thick braid on top of her head. Then she put her shoes on, buckled them tightly, and sat her on the bed until Mama dressed herself.

Mama went into the kitchen to pack the lunch for the girls, for there was very little money for hotdogs at the fair. Packing a lunch would leave money for rides, cotton candy, and a delicious ice cream cone. First, she put pieces of fried chicken and light bread for each girl in a paper sack and placed it in the picnic basket on the table. Then she sliced some cake and put it in the basket, too. The girls liked fruit, so Mama put a jar of her best canned peaches in the basket. Spoons, napkins, and a tablecloth were the last items added. She closed the top of the basket and set it by the door. Mama sent Ginger to sit by the door and watch for the school bus to break over the hill.

Mama checked to see if she had the few cents she managed to save up for the fair safely tucked away in her pocketbook. She kept opening and shutting her pocketbook nervously, making sure she had hidden the money in a safe place. She felt her money again—two dollars in change, to be exact. She fingered it hurriedly, and wrapped and tied it neatly in a handkerchief until she needed it for the fair.

The big yellow school bus burst over the hill. "Heah it comes, Mama!" Ginger yelled. "The bus is coming now! Hurry up and come on before it leaves us!"

"Okay, girls, it's time to go to the fair!" Mama demanded. One by one, the girls spilled out the front door. "Come back here, Mirah, and get that picnic basket!" Mama called. "You won't have any lunch if you don't." The bus halted at the gate, and quickly the door swung wide open and swallowed each girl and Mama within its gaping door. They sat on the big black seats and watched out the window as they passed the houses, trees, and farms near the road. When the bus entered the field where the fair was held, it rolled inside two wide-opened gates, where a tall man in a blue uniform welcomed them in.

As soon as the bus parked, all the girls got out, running wildly. "Come back here!" Mama called to them. "You'll get lost if we don't stick together." She told the girls to stay close to each other, hold hands, and just walk around and look at what's at the fair. She sent them off in pairs so they could look after each other. Mirah and Ginger were to watch out for Nita, and Lola and Greta were to watch Gaye. Mama kept Brownese close by her side, being she was just a toddler and could not keep up with her older sisters. Pointing to the big clock tower, Mama told the girls to meet her at the gate twelve o'clock sharp where they came in and wait until everyone got there before washing their hands and eating lunch.

When the clock struck twelve, the girls began to show up. Lola, Greta, and Gaye were the first ones there. Before spreading the lunch out on the bench, Mama told them to wash their hands and sit down to wait for the other girls. "Be sure to use the 'colored' side of the restroom," she warned. When the girls had finished washing their hands, they all gathered around the bench. Each one grabbed the bag and pulled out a piece of fried chicken, a slice of light bread, and a piece of cake. They spread their lunch on the tablecloth and took turns dipping some peaches to eat with their cake out the quart jar.

Mama told the girls that when they finish eating to go to the toilet and wash their hands again. Tidying up the bench and putting the leftover food into the basket, Mama warned Mirah and Ginger to watch the basket and her pocketbook on the bench while she and Brownese went to the toilet. "You can play nearby," Mama cautioned, "but don't get out of sight of the bench."

Mama returned from the toilet and saw that the girls had scattered nearby to watch a man sitting on a unicycle juggling ten pins while balloons wavered above his head. She called the girls over to her and explained that she only had twenty-five cents a piece for them to spend. Ten cents will get Mirah, Lola, Ginger, and Greta a ride on the Ferris wheel, and ten cents will get Nita and Gaye a hobby-horse ride on the merry-go-round. Brownese and I will sit in one of the chairs on the merry-go-round for ten cents each. Each of you will have fifteen cents left to get a ten cents ice cream cone, and five cents for cotton candy. Only Mirah and Lola can go behind the tent to watch a curio show for ten cents each instead of an ice cream cone.

"Where is my pocketbook?" Mama asked Mirah. "You and Ginger were told to watch my pocketbook on the bench! Now all my money is gone," Mama screeched. "There's nothing to spend at the fair!" The girls looked at Mama in shock as her crying got louder and louder. "All my money is gone!" Mama blasted repeatedly. "There's no money to buy rides! We'll just have to walk around the fair ground to see if we can find out who stole my pocketbook from this bench and every cent I had to my name," Mama scolded.

Mama and the girls walked past the circus elephant and tiger cages, the farm animals, and curio tents. When the stage shows invited them to watch their weird curio shows, all the gazing people went inside, but Mama and the girls just moved on. They pretended they didn't like the shows, while they watched throngs of curious people line up to pay their ten cents for tickets to see the freaks who hastily disappeared behind the curtains.

They stomped around and around the fairground looking for Mama's purse, but they found nothing. Mama told the girls that she saw a lady standing by, Miss Dillah, who watched her out the corner of her eyes as if she wanted to beg for some lunch to eat when we were eating. Mama said to the girls that she must have watched her purse on that bench, too, and as soon as we scattered, she sneaked over to the bench right there and grabbed my pocketbook. "There she goes now," Mama warned. She pointed and shook her finger at the woman. Too afraid to speak about her purse, with all her girls following behind her, Mama followed Miss Dillah for about an hour around the fairgrounds, dragging Brownese with one hand and the picnic basket with the other.

What Mama saw sent her into hysterics. She yelled at the girls and alleged, "She's spending my money on all these rides, and my girls don't even have ten cents to get on the hobby horse." Miss Dillah pretended she didn't even hear Mama and kept her place in line for Ferris wheel rides until her children had ridden twice. "What a shame," Mama announced. "It's such a sin to steal." Miss Dillah paid her no mind because her children were enjoying themselves with Mama's money, and nothing else mattered to Miss Dillah.

The afternoon wore on and on, until it was time to board the yellow school bus for home. The girls loaded on the bus, saying not a word to anyone, with their heads hung down because Mama's pocketbook had been stolen at the fair. No one could tell how empty they felt being at the fair with no money for rides, so their glum faces stared straight ahead while all the other children were laughing and talking happily. The girls just sat there, glued to their seats, too sick at heart to tell anyone about what happened to Mama's pocketbook at the fair. When the bus arrived home and stopped at the gate, Mama pushed all the girls off the bus first. When they were safely on the ground, Lola and Mirah stepped back inside the bus to see why Mama didn't get off. They were shocked when they saw Mama slam Miss Dillah beside the head with the picnic basket and run toward the front door of the school bus. Mama glared at her brazenly and called her a "rogue and thief." She scowled again at Miss Dillah and said, "I'll never have any use for you as long as I live." Exploding with anger, Mama challenged her to step outside the school bus for a fistfight if she didn't like being knocked on the head with the picnic basket. Miss Dillah turned her head and looked out the window, pretending she hadn't been hit with the picnic basket at all and had not heard a word Mama said. Lola and Mirah urged Mama to come on and let's go home. The younger girls, strung in a row, followed behind their older sisters. "Lord, punish her for stealing my money," Mama begged. The girls knew in an instant that Mama was angry and meant every word she said to Miss Dillah. Mama and the girls walked briskly down the path toward the house. With a sorrowful look on their faces, they thought about how rotten the day had been without the rides, ice cream cones, a curio show, and cotton candy. They told Mama they liked the animals at the fair and begged her to take them again next year so they could ride on the Ferris wheel and merry-go-round. But she never did.

The fall days dragged on, waiting for full harvest to begin. The few Indian summer days left were spent drying apples and butterbeans atop the plow shed. Mama needed about a week to can what little vegetables she could glean from the garden before Papa wanted her to help with killing a hog. She hurried to begin preparing jars and gathering vegetables until they were ready to be canned. They had suffered through rationed food stamps brought on by the war, so Mama needed to store away as much canned food as she could for the winter.

Mama had become used to canning fruits and vegetables, and gleaning leftover vegetables from the field to keep the family from going hungry. Many farmers living in the area depended on Papa's family for food to help them get through the cold winter months, mostly those who had no children.

After she ate breakfast, Mama got the jars and rubber rings ready she needed for canning the vegetables. She placed the jars on the kitchen table and found the lids to fit each one before they were scaled and sterilized for processing the vegetables. The rubber rings and tops were washed thoroughly and placed beside each jar.

At dawn before anyone was up and about, Ginger and Greta gathered the butterbeans from the garden that Mama would be canning. They washed the dirt from the beans in a big tub sitting beside the well. Then they each got tin pans from the pantry and shelled the butterbeans before dumping them into a pot of water and setting them on top the cook stove long enough to heat thoroughly. After that, Mama put the beans and a little juice in the boiling hot jars. She added a teaspoon of salt, sugar, and vinegar to keep them fresh inside the jar until they were opened. The lids and rubber seals were screwed on securely and set aside to seal. Jars that don't seal could spoil, so Mama watched them daily to see whether or not they were fermenting right inside the jar. Within a few days, if there was enough evidence, the spoiled jars were opened and emptied and the vegetables thrown away. The empty jars were set aside to wait for the next batch of vegetables to be canned. This canning kept up for the rest of the week until all the vegetables, and fruits if there were any, had been processed.

Before fall was completely over that year, Ginger and Greta returned to helping Papa to harvest the peanuts and cotton. They all wished the winter would arrive quickly because they hated the work in the field harvesting the crops. After the harvest nothing exciting happened to look forward to during the short, chilly fall evenings. Mostly Mama and the girls stayed in the house sitting in front of the fire, and when it got dark, it was time for bed.

All the girls waited for Christmastime when they got the chance to decorate the Christmas tree. Ginger and Greta hitched old stubborn Ginny to the sleigh Papa built for hauling farm equipment. Off to the woods the girls went, with Greta chugging along with Brownese on her lap, to find a perfectly shaped cedar tree, holly with lots of red berries, and mistletoe atop the tall trees.

Getting the mistletoe was more challenging than finding holly berries and the Christmas tree. Ginger, being the strongest girl, could climb trees easily, so she chose the nearest tree that held the mistletoe high atop its branches. Climbing to the top skillfully, Ginger clamped her foot on each tree limb as she climbed toward the branches of mistletoe that were within her reach and perched there. With her long arms, she snapped off the branches of mistletoe and hurled them down to the ground. The girls gathered them in a pile and carefully laid them on the sleigh, trying not to destroy the crystal clear, tiny berries on each limb. After they got the mistletoe home, it was hung above the parlor door where the courting girls hoped for a kiss from the boys, and the grownups wished for good luck.

The holly branches with its bright red berries were hung throughout the house. When no one was watching, the girls pinched a few of the holly berries from its branches. They held their heads back and perched one of these berries on their lips. Then they bet each other who could keep the berry floating above their lips the longest while expelling lungs full of air. The girls thought it took a lot of talent to float a berry, but they had no idea why their oldest sisters, Lola or Mirah, always won the bet.

All the girls joined in to decorate the Christmas cedar tree. They drug it inside the house and set it on a stand in front of the parlor window. One by one they slung icicles on the tree and stuck pieces of cotton deep within its cedar-scented branches. Then they wrapped red and green garland around and around the branches.

While the girls decorated the tree, Mama and Papa went to town to buy items for Santa Claus to leave for the girls. They would return after dark and hide the clothes, fruit, nuts, candy, and raisins in their room until Christmas Eve. The night that Santa Claus was to visit, each girl placed a shoebox underneath her side of the bed with her name on it so Santa Claus could leave special gifts for special girls. When they arose the next morning, they jumped out of bed to examine what Santa had left in their shoeboxes and rushed to see what other large presents were hidden underneath the tree.

Christmas all day long was a great time for a family festive celebration. They all waited to eat the delicious dinner Lola and Mirah would cook Christmas Day. During the week before Christmas, they baked coconut and sweet potato pies. Several pound cakes with assorted icings on each of them were baked as well. Mama set aside one of her premium hams in the smokehouse, soaked the salt out of it, and got it ready to bake.

The turkey Mama purchased from the turkey cages in town was killed and plucked to make ready for Christmas dinner. Mirah had the duty of catching the caged turkey and holding its legs. Lola grabbed the axe and held it in one hand and the turkey's head in the other. She stretched the turkey's neck over a chunk of firewood and chopped down on the neck as hard as she could. Then she let the turkey run wildly around the yard until it dropped dead. Lola dunked the turkey into a pot of boiling water to scald the feathers off. The large and small pin feathers were picked clean from the turkey's skin. Finally, Lola stuck her hand inside the turkey's gut and pulled out the liver, heart, and gizzard. Lola left no part of the turkey to be thrown away.

The giblets were boiled and seasoned with salt, pepper, and sage for the giblet cornbread dressing and set aside to use for stuffing the turkey. The turkey feet were cleaned, skinned, and the nails chopped off. Then they were stewed and seasoned with lots of red pepper. The girls ate them as a delicacy as soon as they were cooked. The drippings from the pan the turkey was baked in were used to make rich, velvet gravy to spread over the mashed potatoes, candied yams, and thick slices of the juicy baked turkey. The Christmas dinner was an occasion when all the family members gathered for a feast.

During the winter months, when the girls were not needed in the field, Mama took that time to examine the dresser drawers to see if their school clothes needed repairing before spring arrived. She would sew new dresses and slips for Lola and Mirah, and use "hand-me-downs" for Ginger and Greta. Mama was sure to warn Nita and Gaye about taking off their shoes and nice dresses until they needed them for school the next day. They only had two or three dresses for school, so they had to wear the same dress for two days before changing it. They wore old ragged and disfigured clothing around the house to play in and went barefoot at home when the weather allowed it.

As soon as Nita and Gaye changed their school clothes, Ginger and Greta always had a hot bowl of soup waiting for them on back of the stove on cold days and various other snacks in the spring. They knew that Nita and Gaye would be hungry and ready to eat when they arrived home from a long day at school.

Spring days were slowly arriving, waiting for the crop seeds to be planted and the hoeing to begin. The few days left before the season arrived were spent tidying up the house and getting the seeds planted for an early summer garden.

Papa alerted Van and Ed two days ago that he would be killing a hog, and they would be needed at home. Papa just didn't like interruptions when he killed a hog, so he got started early in the morning before dawn.

The sow being slaughtered was separated from the other hogs and led to a temporary pen to await the slaughter. Papa summoned Van and Ed to get into the pen, catch the hog, and grab each ear. Then Papa slit the hog's throat and left It to run around and around in the pen until it wobbled off in a daze and fell dead. A hog will squeal as loud as it can when it is being slaughtered, awakening the farmers from way off across the fields. The farmers knew that Papa was killing a hog from the way the squealing sounded, and many of them came to visit Papa on hog-killing day, wishing that a piece of meat or a fresh ham would come their way.

After the hog had been slaughtered, Papa and the boys dumped the carcass into a drum of boiling hot water to scald the hair. Then, Papa and Van laid the hog on top of a table. With a sharp butcher knife, they scraped the hair off the hide. Afterwards, Papa slit a hole through the muscles of the hog's hind legs and rammed a stick through the incisions and hung it up. Next, Papa slit the hog's belly open and emptied the entrails into a twenty-five gallon round tin tub he set on the ground underneath the hog's belly. When this process had been completed, he left the hog hanging until all the blood had drained from its cavity.

The following day, the hog was butchered into quarters for bacon, ribs, hams, and steaks. Papa laid the pork on a slab in the smoke house and dumped lots of salt all over it. When it was ready, the pork was hickory smoked until a brown, crispy rind plastered the skin.

As soon as Mama arose and finished eating breakfast, she took Lola and Mirah, who were staying home from school that day, to help prepare some pots needed for killing the hog. Lola and Mirah took the tin of guts dumped from the hog's belly and toted it under the cottonwood tree in the back yard. There Mama separated all the entrails: intestines, liver, heart, and stomach. The stomach or hog maw and intestines of the hog— Mama called them chitterlings—were placed in yet another tub of water and its bowels emptied.

The hardest part of the hog to prepare was cleaning the maw and chitterlings. The offensive odor spreading from the hog's bowels sent Mama gasping for air, taking her attention away from the cleaning. No one wanted to help Mama with this job, so she seldom asked any of the girls. After Mama finished this grubby task, the chitterlings and hog maw were placed in the black pot Papa set on top the fire on the woodpile to cook until they were tender and juicy.

Using the liver and bits of fat trimmed away from the hams, Mirah ground each piece carefully, seasoned it well, and stuffed it into a few of the chitterlings that she was careful to leave uncooked. Lola looped the stuffed chitterlings, tied the loose ends, and placed them in the smokehouse along with the other hog parts to await the smoking process. Mama used these sausages to season wild cresse salad greens, a delicacy during the spring season. Somehow she knew there would be enough to eat for a few months to come.

After the hog killing was completed, idle days set upon Papa. The spring season of the year was a time that brought unrest. Van and Ed spent the few remaining days before planting the crops hanging around the house and occasionally going to town with Papa. Sometimes they just kept busy looking over the crops that would be ready to chop within a few weeks.

Nita and Gaye walked to elementary school each morning. One arm was loaded with books and writing tablets; the other one lugged their lunch sacks. For lunch, Mama gave them each a biscuit smeared with churned butter and a slice of smoked ham smothered inside. They each carried a mayonnaise jar full of fresh, sweet cow milk. On days when they had no lunch, they joined in with the other children, who got rations of peanut butter, crackers, and maybe an orange or grapefruit.

Mama believed that half of the time Nita and Gaye spent in their one-room schoolhouse down the road was devoted to playing at recess and during the time they walked home from school. She never did hear them talk about the reading, writing, and arithmetic they were learning. Since they never brought schoolwork home, Mama didn't even know whether or not they were studying or learning anything in school.

When Field's Day was held, Nita and Gaye played ball on the girl's softball team and ran relays. At school recess, they practiced softball and played tag and hopscotch games. On rainy days when they couldn't go outside, the children played in the cloak room or hallway. They sat in circles and told stories or played hide-and-go-seek. The older children used the vacant room next door to the classroom to plan activities for the younger children when they were allowed to go outside. The older girls supervised the younger children in fourth and fifth grades, for the teacher had divided them into teams.

The long walk home varied between playing and fighting with other children. There were two routes Nita and Gaye used to get home. One way was called the long way and the other way the shortcut way. They were frequently late arriving to school when they took the long way on the big open road, hoping to get a ride with the teacher and carry some of her books. As soon as school was out, they headed home the short way through the woods and along a rugged path, waving good-bye to the children who, one by one, reached their homes first; but Nita and Gaye had the longest distance to walk.

Gaye and her friend Dottie usually walked home together each afternoon. Today, Dottie was walking just a little ahead of her, so Gaye ran to catch up with Dottie. "Why didn't you wait for me?" Gaye asked.

"Because I heard you telling the other children that my mama and papa were poor, and they didn't have anything for us to eat," Dottie answered, hitting Gaye across the back. Striking back with all her might, Gaye went into a taunting rage and dived on top of Dottie. They rolled over and over on the ground in a vicious fury. The girls and boys who were walking from school caught up with them and stood on the sidelines urging the girls to keep up the fighting. Grabbing Dottie by the collar, Gaye ripped her clothes off her and left her naked, except for her panties. The children sent out a howl and took Dottie's clothes, ran toward the woods, and hid them under some brushes. While getting up off the ground, Dottie grabbed Gaye's leg and sunk her sharp teeth beneath the flesh and spit out blood and flesh at the same time. Seeing what had happened, Gaye tore away from Dottie and ran home as fast as she could, crying and screaming in pain.

When Gaye slammed onto the porch with Nita following her, Mama looked astonished at Gaye and asked, "What have you been doing?" "What's wrong with your leg?" She couldn't figure out what happened to Gaye, and screamed at her to shut up and tell her what had happened. Not being able to calm Gaye, Nita explained to Mama what Dottie had done to Gaye. Mama grabbed the child in her arms and headed for her bedroom.

"Dottie bit me on my leg," Gaye cried. "It hurts, Mama." "Please bathe my leg and put a rag around it so it won't get that blood poison you told us about," Gaye begged. "Please, Mama." Mama undressed Gaye and bathed her leg. Then she rubbed salve on the wounded flesh to soothe the pain. She gave

Gaye a biscuit with jelly inside of it and put her to bed downstairs so she could watch Gaye during the night. Within a few minutes, Gaye stopped crying and went to sleep.

"Lord," Mama whispered. "What kind of monster would bite a child's flesh?"

When Gaye awoke the next morning, her leg was much too sore to walk on. Nita went to school alone, telling everyone she met about Dottie and Gaye's fight. When the teacher heard about the fight, she sent a note to Mama telling her that she expected Gaye to be at school the next day. She wanted to get to the bottom of the news about Gaye and Dottie fighting on the way home from school.

When Gaye returned to school, Dottie had already received her punishment for fighting. Miss Love, the teacher, kept Dottie in her seat each recess for a whole week. At the end of each day, she got fifty licks in the palm of her hand with the ruler and was sent to stand in the corner on one leg for thirty minutes. If Dottie changed her leg she was standing on before Miss Love told her to, she received a whack on the other leg and five more minutes of standing on the same leg.

Gaye was the teacher's pet, but somehow she knew that more of Dottie's type of punishment was coming her way. Sure enough, she was getting the same ruler whacks that Dottie had received, so Gaye asked Nita to wait for her after school. When the other school children had gone, and time had come for Gaye to get fifty whacks in the palm of her hand, Gaye pulled up her dress and took the rag bandage off her leg to show the teacher where Dottie had bitten her. Seeing the raw flesh lying bare on Gaye's leg, the teacher stood there in shock. She opened her mouth wide open, and yelled, "Oh, my Lord! Does that hurt?" She walked back to her desk and set the ruler down in the corner. Gaye began to sob painfully, afraid of what her teacher would do about her and Dottie fighting. Gaye crawled into Miss Love's lap and laid her head on her shoulder. She waited for her to say something soothing to her. Gently, Miss Love wiped the tears away from Gaye's eyes and sent her home to Mama. Gaye never did get the whacks in her hand that Dottie got, but the scar from the wound where Dottie bit her on her right leg lasted for the rest of her life.

During the remaining spring days, the girls studied hard in the evening after school whenever they didn't have housework to do. The lamp light was mostly too dull for them to study by after darkness fell. Besides, kerosene oil was scarce; it cost too much, and each family was rationed a portion for home use. What little was available in the one or two lamps the family owned was needed to see how to cook and eat supper. Other activities would have to wait until morning light. Many times when the kerosene got so low in the lamps, the lamp light just went out, sending everyone off to bed in the dark. The next morning Papa would scramble together a few cents and go to the store to buy more kerosene. He kept the oil wicks trimmed and cleaned, hoping the kerosene would last longer. Papa warned the girls, too, about wasting the lamp light and cleaning the globes so they would give out more light. Otherwise, kerosene hardly lasted long enough to see the week through before it was time to buy more. The ones who were to use lamplight to study by were Lola and Mirah; however, they did most of their homework at school in study hall. The one lamp in the house that was allowed to stay on all the time was in Mama and Papa's room, and it had to be shared with the entire household when the kerosene got low. Whenever the lamp was needed in another room, it had to be carried off to that room and brought back promptly to Mama and Papa's room when it was no longer needed. Often Mama and Papa just used the light from the fireplace during the wintertime when they got ready for bed and let the lamp burn alternately in one of the girl's room.

During the spring months, Mama busied herself in the house the last few days before summer arrived, for she knew that within a few days, hoeing the crops would begin. Nearly all summer long, she and the girls were back in the fields, hoeing the half-mile-long rows of cotton and peanuts. They always tried to hoe the crops as well as they could, keeping the wire grass and noxious weeds from overtaking the plants. Besides, keeping the grass away promised a higher yield during the fall harvest. After the chopping was finished, Papa and the boys laid-by the crops to grow until they reached full maturity. This summer was no different from the rest of them.

Summer had come and gone, though, before the treacherous rain began. The tree leaves had put on their array of colorful foliage, letting everyone know that fall season was in full swing. Rainy days in the farmland had started up. Rain is never welcomed at all during fall season, but the field-workers are glad for one day's rest away from the toil. One day away from the field produces laziness and drains strength from the workers, Papa would say. Worse than that, when the rain comes, the grass in the field grows greener. Just two days of rainy weather make it nearly impossible for the crops to bear unless they are plowed again. Papa hoped the rain would end soon that morning, and by the afternoon they could begin to plow the crops and get them ready for harvest. No such thing happened; it just rained and rained and rained.

Well into the fourth day of drenching rain, Papa realized that a flood had set in. The rainwater in the furrows where the crops were plowed had quickly gotten level with the hills of cotton and peanuts; and the water was beginning to flow toward gullies, forming deep trenches in each row. Hidden underneath these furrows were peanuts and cotton plants, their tops barely peeking above the water. The peanut roots were soaked, exposing the young, tender nuts above the ground. Premature knotty, seedy cotton bolls fell to the ground while others sagged on the stalks from the rain that left them battered. The wind had blown the cornstalks sideways, leaving the heavy ears of corn flopping and sagging above the trenches.

Papa paced back and forth to the door, but the rain never stopped. During early mornings and evenings, and intervals when the pouring rain waited for the sun to set, Papa, Ed, and Van put on their coats and boots and dashed toward the barn to feed the mules, cows, and hogs. Before they could hardly finish, and before night set in, the rain began again.

During the night the rain was worse than during the day. Lying in bed, Papa could hear the roof leaking, producing slow splatter drips that started a steady ping, plop, plop. He darted skillfully up and down the stairs with buckets, trying to find where the roof leaks were hiding so he could catch them in the half a dozen pails he had lined up on the porch. After Papa found where the entire roof leaks were coming from, he set buckets underneath them to catch the leaking water. He vowed to mend the old tin-top roof, but not now. He really forgot about the leaking roof until the rain started again. He promised himself to buy several sheets of tin to mend the roof in the fall when he sells the crops. Creeping back to bed, Papa was careful not to awaken anyone. He went back to sleep as the ceiling continued its drip, drip, drip. Papa prayed for a clear day to come in the morning.

Stepping outside into the October morning sun, Papa was anxious to find out what crops he could salvage after the flood that lashed them without letting up. Many farmers just gave up and, painfully, watched their crops float away and were too down-trodden to look toward the fields. When the rain was all over, Papa and the boys walked over each crop they had planted, looking at the ravages the flood had left behind. Sadly, each crop they planted barely had anything left to harvest, neither were there any vegetables left to eat in the garden. It was as if an ocean had flowed through the fields, destroying everything in its path or plastered it to the ground. In some fields only the tips of the crops could be seen floating and wavering above water.

Papa did not know how many animals had drowned in the flood, but one thing was for sure; he had lost several livestock. One of the calves floated above the water, confused in the watery, soggy tomb. A couple of piglets were trapped and drowned in their pens; their bodies floated atop the water. One pig had gotten a swollen belly and was forced to stretch out topsy-turvy on its back. It, too, would soon die.

The rain had gone now, at least for a while, but no one was anxious to get back to hard fieldwork. There was little to be done, though, for most of the crops were destroyed. Papa and the boys would try to harvest what little was left, with the hope that the yield would bring in a few dollars. Only a miracle could produce a good harvest this fall.

Papa set his mind to thinking how he could pay all the debts he owed from the year before. As far as he could figure, hardly any changes had been made in the family's income. He owed for each peanut and cotton seed he had planted, and the bags of fertilizer needed to make the seeds spring up from underneath the ground.

The peanuts had to be shocked in the fields to dry. As soon as the ground became dry, Papa and the boys set out early each morning, turning over the soil beneath the peanuts and uprooting them.

Mama and the girls walked behind the plows and vigorously shook as much dirt as they could from each peanut root. The vines were carefully lifted and shocked tightly around each of the thousand poles set in the rows. If it rained again, it would soak the vines, but the peanuts would remain dry. They stayed on the shocks from five to six weeks during the fall days, until the big machines came along to thresh them. Then the peanuts were bagged and taken to the market and sold. Papa usually kept some of the sacks of peanuts for seeds for the coming year, but this year he needed to sell them all for cash money because the crops were short. The seed peanuts would have to be bought early in the spring.

Mama sent the girls to savage what few peanuts had been left on the ground during the harvesting and threshing. She hoped they could find a few bags more of peanuts that the rain had ripped from the vines and left in the field or that had not rotted but had fallen to the ground as they were shaken. The girls raked the peanuts into piles, gathered them in bags, and laid them on a slab in the crib house to dry. The girls liked picking up peanuts because they made good winter snacks, once they were dried and roasted.

While the peanuts were drying, cotton-pickin' season was in full gear, so the long rows of nappy, seedy cotton swaged in the field waiting to be picked. With a guano sack strung across their backs, Mama and the girls drug those cotton bags up and down the rows, picking the popped-open bolls until the stalks were bare. Their hands were scratched, sore, and sometimes bleeding from the pricks and jabs of the gnarled cotton bolls; but they trudged on, knowing full well that the cotton had to be picked before the rain came again.

The more cotton Mama and the girls stuffed into those guano sacks, the heavier they were to drag up and down the rows. Emptying the stuffed sacks into the wagon waiting at the end of the rows was the only relief their shoulders and bent-over, aching backs got. When the wagon was filled with loose cotton, off to the cotton gin Papa went, hoping that the merchant who compressed his cotton into bales would buy them from him at a good price. All hope drained from Papa when he realized that the rain caused the seeds to embed themselves deeply within the knotty bolls of cotton. The rain had done more damage to the cotton than he had imagined.

Mama never forgot to plant purple hull field peas between the cotton stalks where the cotton failed to grow. The peas that withstood the flood and dried in the field were picked and stored for soup, and the few that had not dried were shelled and thrown into a cooking pot with a ham hock that was simmering on back of the stove. A pan of buttermilk cornbread to eat with the peas made this meal a delicacy that everyone loved.

The white potatoes were dug and put into the crib to dry before eating during the winter months. Had they lingered in the muddy ground too long, they would rot. Papa ordered the girls to put the potatoes in a bin he made in the crib house so they would be within easy reach for cooking. A bushel of corn was taken to the gristmill. It was ground into cornmeal and used for hot, steaming cornbread. The sweet potatoes were dug and dried. Afterwards, they were put inside hills of straw to keep warm during the snowy and freezing weather.

Papa knew that what few repairs the farm machinery needed before next harvest would cost far more than what he owed out. He would continue on, though, trying not to get the farm too heavily in debt, but he knew that the amount he owed the merchants would keep him bound in debt for another long planting and harvesting season. Since the flood had nearly ruined everyone's harvest, the merchants took pity on the farmers. They accepted half of the payment that the farmers normally owed in loans and waited for the next harvest to collect the balance of the farm debts. Papa was thankful he could pay at least half of the money he had borrowed. The other half would be used to keep his family living throughout the cold winter months and into spring when it was planting season again.

Late fall days when the farm work scaled down, Mama took a break from house work and walked up to the mailbox at the end of the path to pick up from the box the mail the postman left. She had not seen him stop, but she heard his car starting up and taking off again. Usually her brisk steps took her to the mailbox and returned her swiftly after she had collected the mail, but this morning she had a piece of strange mail in her hands. Slowing her pace, and taking each step deliberately, Mama came to an abrupt halt right in the middle of the path. Holding the piece of white paper before her glaring eyes, she began to tremble uncontrollably. She held in her hand a letter from the U. S. government, and she read each word slowly. After she had read each line again, mounting outrage entered her and choked off her breath. Stepping up her pace, Mama rushed into the house and hid the letter underneath the pillow on her bed. "I won't tell a soul about this letter until after supper, and the news should be heard by the whole family," Mama thought. "Yes, we will assemble on the back porch and I will give the family this horrible news." She continued to work around the house until nightfall, but her mind kept returning to that letter. When the opportunity came, she told Papa that Van had received a letter from the U.S. government and had been drafted to leave home as soon as he could for the war. The news left Papa both stunned and confused, but Mama knew that they would have to obey the summons.

After they had all eaten a big supper, Mama gathered the children around her on the back porch and read the letter aloud. She clutched the letter between her trembling fingers and held her breath between each word she spoke. "Van, you are in class 1-A, and must report to the train depot to be processed for joining the U. S. Army." The girls sat there staring at Mama and wondering what on earth she was talking about. All the family wanted to know what will happen to Van. They worried that he was summoned to leave them to go to a far off place—only God knows where. Van jumped to his feet and cried with fear. He spoke of the boys who left for the army and were shipped to Germany. No one had heard from them again. Van was afraid this would happen to him.

"I won't go," Van yelled, trembling from fright. "Some of the boys around here never returned from the war." Trying to console him, Papa explained to him that he was needed to help serve his country and to keep it free from the enemy. Surely he wanted to go to the army. Everyone was afraid of the war except Papa. "When do I report?" Van asked.

Lifting the paper to her eyes, "Monday is the quickest time you can go," Mama said. Silence and sobbing grief swept over the family sitting there in a fixed daze. "The other girls will help with the farm work," Mama explained. "You'll come back when the war is over, and we will be just fine while you are away." Mama began to pray and lift her eyes toward the sky, asking God to protect her son from harm when he goes to some foreign country no one knows anything about. She took Van's leaving real hard, but it was harder trying to keep her feelings to herself.

As soon as Mama cleared the tears from her weeping eyes and raised her head, she pointed toward the night sky across the hill where the old, gnarled cedar tree stood. "Look at the light!" she screamed. Everyone looked up just in time to see a bright light shoot up from the ground. It raised itself over the hill and flared upward, lighting the starry sky. It left a path a half mile wide as it streaked across the field above the towering oak trees. It flashed again and faded out of sight. Frightened by what she and Papa had just seen, Mama rushed the girls off to bed. She pushed and urged them along and forced them to unglue themselves from standing in their tracks amazed. Frozen to their seats, Mama and Papa stayed on the porch, hoping they could get another glimpse of the flashing light, but nothing appeared.

Mama continued to stretch her arms toward heaven in prayer, and Papa joined her. They gazed toward the cedar tree far into the night, stretching their eyes desperately to see anything that could explain the flashing light they had just seen.

Papa was ranting wildly now, and just as soon as he turned to go into the house, the flash of light appeared again. This time it left a bright, howling streak of light, shooting upward out of the ground. In the light they thought they saw the image of poor little Walden, crying and wailing. He was sucking his thumb, full of fright and terror. No sooner had the flash of light appeared than his frail body vanished in the darkness. "Maybe Van's leaving home means bad luck!" Mama said.

"No!" Papa replied. "He will be in the U. S. Army." Papa convinced Mama that the army will take good care of Van. "The light streaking across the field means good luck that Walden is trying to lead us to, instead of bad luck," Papa argued. "Just suppose there is good luck under that old cedar tree," Papa wondered. "I will go to town Monday with Van to see if I can learn more about the army." Papa told Mama that after he finishes with Van, he will discuss this light they saw with someone in town and try to find out what it means when lights rise up from the ground on folks' property and flash out of sight across the night sky. Papa wanted to know if some of those old slaves had hid treasures under that gnarled cedar tree. He had heard of folks who buried treasure, and the notion that his land held buried treasure got stuck in his head.

Papa's mind struggled long into the night over why in the world this light appeared to them and then faded out across the black sky right before their eyes. He couldn't for the life of him figure out all this. He decided for sure that he would go into town and discuss this sighting.

Early Monday morning, Papa and Van arose, ate breakfast, and hurried to the barn lot. They quickly hitched up Lucy and Ginny to the wagon, and took off down the road to town. Papa took Van straight to the train depot, where he was examined and reclassified for the army.

Van never returned home that day. He and a dozen other young boys were examined in a holding room, given a ticket to ride, and lined up to wait for the train. Van only saw one other boy he knew, Winfield, who lived over on the next farm. He had seen him once or twice before, but he really didn't know him well. He wondered if Winfield was going to the army, too.

Papa remembered that he had heard some years ago of a man who was going over the countryside hunting for buried treasure and had set himself up in business in one of the hardware stores in town. He wanted to meet this man and talk to him, so he walked right into the store to find him and to learn more about whether or not it might be buried treasure on his farm. "Oh, yes!" "There is something strange going on here," Papa thought. He noticed a man sitting in a chair under a sign that read: "Get buried treasure dug up on your land for a small fee." He stared so hard at the man that he motioned to Papa to step right up and talk to him. Papa panted as he staggered toward the man, but he calmed down enough to explain that he had seen a light on his property the other night flash up from underneath an old cedar tree of his up the path from his house. "I believe some buried treasure is there," Papa convinced the man.

The man wore a nametag around his neck that read: "See Mr. Toms for all your buried treasure." He sprang from his chair and thrust out his hand to meet Papa's in such a strong grip that Papa nearly dropped to his knees in pain. "How anxious this man seems," Papa mumbled. He told Mr. Toms his story about the light flashing from the ground.

"I can search for your buried treasure using a crooked metal pole," he told Papa. "When do you want me to start?"

"What do you know about this flashing light thing?" "How much do you charge?" Papa asked all in one breath before Mr. Toms could answer his first question.

"Oh, I ask for a third of the treasure we find, and you keep the rest," Mr. Toms explained. "If I don't find any treasure, my fee is twenty-five cents an hour for digging and the time I spend staring into empty holes." With this in mind, Papa blurted out the directions to his farm and asked Mr. Toms if he could show up the next day to start.

Mr. Toms quickly assured Papa that after dusk is the best time for digging. "This here metal pole shows a bright red or green light when we come upon the treasure at night," he continued explaining. "If we work by daylight, the red and green lights don't show up as well; besides, daylight attracts nosey folks who might just come looking for your treasure themselves." He stared straight into Papa's face and told him point blank that news will spread quickly and travel far and wide about your lucky spot if someone else finds out about this treasure. He confided in Papa that only the two of them should dig for the treasure at night. Then, only you and I will know about your lucky spot.

Papa hesitated no longer and hoped that Mr. Toms wouldn't change his mind and disappoint him. He hurried to the stables where he left Lucy and Ginny tied to the wagon. After hitching them up to the wagon, Papa yelled, "Git up!" and trotted them briskly toward home. When he arrived, Mama rushed outside to hear the news. "Where is Van?" she asked.

"Van was shipped off today," Papa said. He told Mama that a load of boys got on the train heading for the army already to some town we don't know about. They just snatched up my boy and packed him into the train along with a dozen other boys, and it struggled up the track as it left the depot. Van hardly had time to say good-bye to his papa before the train sped up the track. You should have seen the empty, sad eyes staring at the boys; folks didn't say a word, too scared to even speak. Slowly, they lifted their arms to wave good-bye and fell to their knees in prayer and grief as the train disappeared up the track.

Papa barely made it in time to see Van off. They told him his wait wouldn't be long and that he passed his exam quickly. The army man said they needed strong men like Van. Papa explained to Mama that the army people told him there is no way of knowing where Van is going unless Van writes us a letter letting us know where he is.

Mama's eyes grew teary when she heard what Papa said. She went to her room and closed the door. She cried, sniffled, and started praying about the emptiness she felt because Van was taken away from her, and she didn't know where he was going. Papa followed her into the room and tried to make her stop crying, but Mama couldn't stop long enough to listen.

Later that evening, when Mama had stopped crying, Papa explained to her how he came across a man who thinks that we have buried treasure on our land because of the light that we saw flashing toward the sky night before last. I asked him to come over tomorrow evening before dark to dig for the treasure. He convinced me that the light we saw meant buried treasure on the property. There was nothing else for Mama to think except that the man knew better than they did. The flash of light up from beneath the earth was a sign of buried treasure instead of an answer from God that their son would be safe in the army. They hoped it would be both, but they would have to wait and see.

Papa sat around all the next day, hoping and praying he would not let on to Mama that he was too scared and tense to find out whether or not they would find any buried treasure on their land. He didn't tell Mama about his lurid feelings for fear she would become impatient, too. He could look into her pleading eyes and see that she felt the same way.

Very few words passed between Mama and Papa as they tried to go about their busy work around the house the night Mr. Toms was coming to dig for the treasure. As soon as dusk fell, they sat on the back porch and turned their teary eyes toward the path. They just sat there staring and waiting until dusk turned to darkness and showed the bright lights of Mr. Toms' jalopy, coming hastily down the path. Their eyes followed the car's head-lights until it parked in the back yard.

As soon as his jalopy came to a halt, Mr. Toms jumped out the car and ran toward the porch. He grabbed Papa by the arm and pulled him down the steps to greet him and to force him toward his car. He told Papa he had gotten all the equipment he needed to dig with, and began unloading a long, shiny, crooked pole. He laid it on the grass underneath the cottonwood tree. Papa grabbed his pickaxe nearby that he would need later to help unearth the treasure and set it beside the porch steps. Mr. Toms unloaded what looked like a flat round reflecting mirror with a bulb attached underneath its glass plate. He laid that piece out beside the pole and fastened the two of them together. "This ought to hold the plate steadily," Mr. Toms remarked. He banged it forcefully on the ground.

Papa grabbed the pickaxe and the crooked pole and led Mr. Toms toward the hill beneath the cedar tree where he thought he had seen the flashing light appear and where the treasure might be buried. Just as Papa reached the edge of the yard, he turned his face toward the lamplight on the porch and caught a glimpse of Mama shooing the girls from the porch and chasing them off to bed. They had all gathered there to watch Papa and Mr. Toms, with their foreheads, noses, and lips pressed tightly against the porch screen, which held them fixed in a frozen mask. "Go to bed and get off this porch," Mama yelled. "Be quiet, too, and don't disturb your papa."

Papa led Mr. Toms to the exact spot where he thought he had seen the light shoot up from the ground. "Start looking here," Papa said. No sooner had these words left Papa's mouth than Mr. Toms grabbed the long, crooked pole from Papa's hand and thrust it onto the cold, bare ground. Using his trickery, he told Papa exactly what he was doing.

"When the green light pops on and begins to flicker, it means that treasure is buried somewhere in the distance," Mr. Toms warned Papa. "When the red light pops on and begins to flicker, it means that we are standing right above the very spot where some gold coins are buried," he added.

At the least faint sighting of a red light, the two men became anxious and began digging with the pickaxe and shovel as fast as they could, long and hard. But the harder they dug, the fainter the red light grew, until it finally turned green again, without even giving at least one flicker. This process left Papa frantically defeated as he gazed into each empty hole.

Papa followed behind Mr. Toms blindly, ready to shove the pickaxe into the earth at the first sign of a flickering red light that heralded from the end of the crooked pole. They dug on and on into the night for hours, watching and following where the mirror kept flashing a green light and a red light but refused to flicker at least one time, letting Papa know whether or not treasure was buried in that spot. The searching kept up until dawn. By then, Papa was so tired he could barely drag the pick-axe behind Mr. Toms, who carried the crooked pole. Mr. Toms raced against the dawn, darting aimlessly from first one spot that promised to hold treasure and then to another, following where the mirror kept flashing green and red from place to place. Again, the red light kept flashing but gave no flickering sign letting them know treasure was buried in the spot they were standing above. Each instance turned up nothing. Papa tried with all his might to dig holes with the pickaxe and keep up with Mr. Tom's crooked pole, too. As the big yellow sun burst above the tree tops and looking back over his enchanted field, Papa counted over fifty different empty holes that had been dug. As dawn drew nearer, the digging stepped up its pace.

Disappointed at having found no buried treasure at all, Mr. Toms finally motioned to Papa to quit digging. Papa fixed his eyes on the field, hoping he could determine if any spots had been left that needed to be dug up. "There's much more ground left to run the crooked pole over," Mr. Toms assured Papa. "There's much more ground left to find just the perfect spot that holds that treasure, too." He Told Papa that he would be back the next night and try to hunt for the treasure again.

Quickly Mr. Toms disconnected the mirror from the pole, unscrewed the bulb and turned off the switch. He shook off the caked dirt, walked down the path, and loaded the crooked pole into his car. When Papa stared back over the field, Mr. Toms shoved Papa's pickaxe in the back seat and pushed it underneath the other junk hidden there. In an instant, he jumped into his car and fled down the path toward the road, racing the motor as it sputtered and choked hurriedly over the bumpy path. Mr. Toms disappeared from Papa's sight as he faded into the dawn.

"What had all this been for?" Papa asked himself hopelessly. The flashing green and red light didn't turn up any treasures at all. They came close to a spot, but the red light just turned back to green, and it wouldn't even flicker a single time. All this work was for nothing. Papa was the specter of an old critter and was at a loss to figure out why he wasted all his effort.

Walking into the house, listening, Papa didn't hear a sound. When he entered the room where Mama was, she had just gotten out of bed and was sitting in front of the fireplace. Her pleading eyes stretched wide open and looked up at Papa. She waited to hear good news about what they had found. "We had no luck," Papa said. "We couldn't locate any buried treasure out there, so we will try again tomorrow night." Exhausted from all the holes left in his field he had dug, Papa peeled off his muddy shoes and dusty overalls he was wearing, flung himself across the bed and dozed off into a deep slumber.

Papa waited aimlessly for Mr. Toms to show up the next evening. After midnight, he didn't wait any longer for him and went to bed without digging for the treasure again.

Early the next morning, he remembered that Mr. Toms didn't show up at all last night. Papa jumped out of bed and dressed himself quickly. He walked up the path to the field where they had dug for the treasure the night before. Standing there surrounded by all those gaping holes in the ground, he stumbled upon one hole that was at least four feet deep. "What has happened here?" He wondered. The fresh soil appeared to have been dug with a shovel and pick axe, but Papa remembered that Mr. Toms didn't have a pickaxe. Gazing into the empty hole more closely, Papa grabbed two or three worthless coins spilled on the outside of the hole, barely visible above the dirt.

Mr. Toms lied to Papa when he told him the green and red lights would flicker, yet the crooked pole holding the light bulb in place wasn't supposed to flicker at all. It just flashes red when there is treasure and green when treasure is close by. "Had Mr. Toms come back in the night and unearthed the treasure?" Papa wondered. Standing there stunned and frozen in his tracks, his strength slowly drained from his legs as he sank his eyes into the depths beneath him.

Jumping into the hole, Papa began scratching the earth around him with his bare hands. He could see that a wooden crate partly covered with soil had been lifted from its bed. Straining his eyes, he noticed the lid was rotten and cracked. With what little strength Papa had left, he ripped the planks completely off the rotten crate and thrashed his hand around inside until it gripped an old rusty tin can lodged there. Prying it open, his fingers groped inside the can while hoping to find the bur-

ied treasure or some coins that might still be lingering there. Finding nothing, he hurled the rusty tin
can back into the old wooden crate, climbed out
the hole, and stood there staring down in it. With
the side of his boot, he raked some dirt over the
hole, hoping no one would notice that it had been
freshly dug.

Papa knew for sure that Mr. Toms had sneaked
back during the night and stole the buried treasure while he fell asleep on the bed lying next to
Mama. If Mr. Toms didn't steal the treasure, he
just might have shared the story with someone
who stole out to his place before dawn and dug
up the treasure. Papa walked aimlessly down the
path toward the house, dispirited, barely glancing
up to see where he was headed. Thinking to himself about Mr. Toms, a crook and thief in the night,
Papa became more puzzled and asked himself,
"Why didn't we ever see a red light flicker among
all those flashing red lights? Yes, Mr. Toms actually
told me a red flickering light meant that gold coins
were buried in the spot."

Papa was too dumb-founded and empty-hearted to even ask Mr. Toms about the treasure, knowing full well what the answer would be. He thought it strange, anyway, that Mr. Toms never showed up the next night, as he promised, to dig for the buried treasure again; and Papa, having confided in him, was too disgusted and astounded to even ask why he never came.

The next month, Papa fixed his own crooked pole and gathered some tools to search for buried treasures, if any were left, and went over the entire field again trying to remember the places where the lights flashed red. As he was gathering his digging tools, he needed his pickaxe Mr. Toms had stolen, but he didn't let it stop him. On and on he searched, turning up no buried treasure.

During the years that followed, the only satisfaction Papa got was the fact that as blindly as the night had coughed up the buried treasure, he had been tricked out of his fortune by a thief. Papa never shared Mr. Toms' trickery with Mama. Like the gold coins he searched deep within the holes,

Papa kept the secret about the gold coins buried deep within his memory. When he got up the nerve to inquire in town about Mr. Toms, Papa was the only one who had not gotten wind of the treasure rumor going around the countryside: "Mr. Toms and another man found buried gold coins a year or so ago in a field somewhere on a farm down south and have since fled town on a freight train, never to be seen again. They settled in a town way up north where nobody knew their names and couldn't remember them if they tried."

Papa was stunned; he just hung his head and moped around for months to come without letting on to anyone that he was the man Mr. Toms robbed and was too ashamed and helpless to do anything about the thievery. The deep scowl on Papa's face gave away the secret that he was the man who got gypped out of the treasure on his own land.

Hoping the flashing light would reappear and lead him to buried treasure in another field some-where beneath the stubby cotton roots, Papa's mind grew deep beneath the soil, fastening itself onto the memories of buried hope. As quickly as the flashing light disappeared in the night sky, his dreams of buried treasure escaped from his head, never to be thought of again.

Defeated by the loss of the treasure that was never to be, Papa devoted much time to forgetting the episode with Mr. Toms and threw himself into the bleak winter months ahead. He took to going into town frequently with the wagon and mules. There wasn't much to do in town during the winter months except to stand in front of the hardware store to chat with other farmers who were victims of the flood. The storefront was a meeting place to share losses, profits, and to talk about the months ahead.

Papa would get up early in the morning and take Ed with him. There was very little money to purchase anything from the hardware store, but Papa always found a quarter or fifty cents to purchase small items like screws or bolts that were needed to repair the wagon or plow. At other times, when he had five dollars or more, he bought a sack of flour, salt fish, and some chunks of stewing beef. He really didn't go into town to buy any food; he just wanted it to look that way, especially since Mama always asked him why he needed to go in the first place.

What little money left over after Papa bought the items he needed was spent buying a pint of his favorite whisky to drink in the wagon on the way home. When Papa was not looking, or after he had taken one or two drinks, Ed thought it funny to sneak a swig of whisky from Papa's bottle, which caused him to become giddy and silly. Sometimes Ed even hid Papa's bottle in the wagon from him and waited for Papa to look for it. If Papa could not find his bottle, he accused Ed of moving it and not giving it back to him.

By the time Papa landed home, he had become good and tipsy. Mama would watch him light down from the wagon. As soon as he did, she could tell if he had been drinking whisky from the way he was walking. It was because of his drinking during these trips to town that sent Mama and Papa into frenzied arguments. This griping, mumbling, and arguing back and forth continued throughout the night.

Mama was frightened whenever Papa drank whisky, and often wondered how he could keep old Lucy and Ginny on the dark road. She didn't like the way he was staying out with Ed all day and far into the night, especially since the wagon with Papa in it had been hit by a truck on the busy highway a couple of years ago. The wagon had no lights in the dark, so a mule and wagon on a busy highway created panic in Mama's heart.

During the winter months when money was so scarce, Papa needed to borrow money from the white merchants, supposedly to buy farm supplies, but Mama knew that a lot of the money was squandered on whisky. Every Saturday when Papa came back from town with the smell of whisky on his breath, Mama accused him of being drunk. Came Sunday morning, Papa brushed himself off, and he and Mama went to church. They respected each other even though they argued each time Papa had a drink. They never passed a lick between them; they just argued and fussed all the time.

Mama tried to get Papa to stop drinking whisky. When he had not been to town, they got along well together and didn't argue with each other. They acted as though they were in love and concerned about the welfare of the family and farm. But once Saturday rolled around, or days during the week when Papa went to town, for that matter, the girls knew what to expect: Mama and Papa arguing long hours throughout the night.

Mama was at a loss to know what had caused Papa to start drinking like he did. She couldn't figure out if it was the flood or the buried treasure that occupied his mind and made him feel like a failure. Anyway, he never liked to take Mama with him to town anymore because she would not let him wander off alone to drink whisky with his buddies.

When Papa took Mama to town the following Saturday, What made him so irritable once he got to town was that Mama made him promise to return her home early in the afternoon. She'd put her foot down, telling Papa she had to get home before dark. They left early in the morning before day-break when the traffic was light and before the sun beamed down on their heads. Mama also figured that going home in the evening after the sun goes down in the summer time makes the ride more comfortable, but she was afraid of the darkness.

Sometimes she and Papa were gone as long as six hours, even though that length of time was far too long for Mama to stay away from home. There were the young girls and older ones, too, to care for. If Mama wasn't there, the older ones, especially Lola and Mirah, would take to bossing the younger girls around. When they disobeyed, it gave Lola and Mirah an excuse to lash out at the younger girls as if they were their mama, and coax them into fighting and arguing with each other.

Ed would walk up to the gate at the end of the path, trying to catch a ride to town just as soon as the wagon wound around the curve and out of sight of the house. He hung out with his friends all day when Mama and Papa were gone, and returned just before dusky dark. Somehow Ed knew when it was time for Mama and Papa to leave town and arrive home. That way, he could beat Mama and Papa home by only a few minutes, knowing full well that he had been told not to leave the house. Whenever Papa asked him about leaving home, he had only walked to the store and stayed an hour.

Lola and Mirah's favorite thing to do as soon as the wagon carrying Mama and Papa to town was out of sight was to bake cookies and make peanut brittle candy. To do this baking, they used some of Papa's seed peanuts leftover from the harvest. They were not allowed to use sugar because it was rationed, and they hardly had enough to last for a month at mealtime. If they made cookies, Lola sent the young girls to the hens' nests to scour for eggs. They could use the flour without Mama noticing that some of it was gone, but she kept her eggs counted. There was no way Lola and Mira could use them without her knowing it. Whatever it was that they got into while Mama and Papa were gone was not allowed when they were at home.

The younger girls were very useful when the cooking was going on. They were told to stand by the door to watch for the wagon returning from town with Mama and Papa. They were to warn them in time so they could clean up the mess they made cooking. For this little favor, the younger girls were promised a piece of the peanut brittle candy after it was made, and two cookies each after they were done, but not before they promised not to tell Mama what they had done when she returned home.

The flour on the kitchen floor had to be cleaned up and the pans washed and put away so Mama couldn't tell if they had been baking. If the peanut brittle didn't turn out right, Lola ordered Nita and Gaye to bury it in the cotton patch. When the cookies were too hard to eat, they offered them to the scraggly hound dog sitting in the yard begging for a measly crumb of bread. If the dog didn't eat the cookies, they would be buried also. It was always after they had done the things Mama warned them not to do before any of the chores were done.

Lola and Mirah were told to sweep the yard and chop the grass and weeds from the flower beds. Before they could sweep the yard, though, the girls discovered that they needed to make a trip to the edge of the field and lop off a few limbs from the dogwood tree for brush brooms. These were ideal for sweeping the yard because the branches were leafy and tough, and they remained sturdy, longer than elm or oak limbs. If the yard had not been swept clean, the girls were afraid Mama surely would spank each one of them.

When they went to get the brush broom, they had to take the younger girls, too, before Mama and Papa returned from town and caught them home alone. Lola and Mirah were afraid to leave the younger girls at home alone, especially since Lola had scaled the gypsy hag who wanted to run away with their baby sister. Besides, words spread quickly when Mama and Papa are seen alone in town without the girls. Many unsuspecting incidents occur on the farm when girls are left unattended for long hours. Mama had talked to the older girls on many occasions about staying together and not leaving the younger two girls in the house alone. Even when they only went to the edge of the fields, they had to drag Brownese and Gaye along, too, often with them in their arms or on their backs, for lack of better ways to carry them. Mama also had warned them not to go to the door when strange cars showed up in the yard. They were to lock the screen doors and pretend no one was home. Wanderers who came by the house would notice no one home and leave without talking to anyone.

Mama would be disappointed to know they did not weed the flower beds. Looking for brush brooms took up most of the time, especially when they had to take Gaye and Brownese with them.

When Mama and Papa returned from town, the girls all rushed to the wagon to see what they had bought. The girls were promised goodies if they behaved themselves and did as they were told, so Mama made sure that each one got a toy or something to wear or keep from the five-and-dime store. Before Mama could hardly get out of the wagon,

Lola and Mirah jumped into the wagon and seized the packages from Mama. They took them into her room and spread them on the bed. Then they all sat around on the floor while Mama opened each one's paper sack.

The first paper sack Mama opened was a wide bright ribbon to tie a bow on Brownese's bronze curls. Then she found a compact for Mirah and a comb and mirror for Lola. Ginger and Greta both received a pair of socks to match their dresses. Nita and Gaye's eyes popped wide open when Mama pulled two big surprises for them out of the paper bag. Nita got a shiny, bright, golden locket to wear around her neck, and Gaye got two silver barrettes shaped like hearts to fasten onto her black, long, shiny plaits that bounced all over her head as she danced with joy. After getting all their surprises, Mama pushed the girls from her room and told them to put their presents away until it was time to wear them. "Put your things away and wear them to Sunday school Sunday," Mama called upstairs to the girls.

Mama changed her dressy clothes she wore to town and promised to cook the girls a delicious supper, since some of the chores were done and the girls had behaved themselves while she and Papa were gone—so she thought. No one told of the peanut brittle and the cookies Lola and Mirah made while Mama and Papa were in town, unless some of the younger girls became angry with their older sisters. They vowed, though, that no one would tattletale at the supper table. They hoped that by suppertime they would be hungry enough not to force themselves to eat, but the cookies they ate were not fit to eat; they made their stomachs ache and had to be buried in the cotton patch.

After Papa changed his clothes, he made a fire in the cook stove so Mama could cook supper. She waited patiently for the cooking eyes on top the stove to get hot before letting Papa wander off to feed the mules, hogs, and cows. They would discuss further the gossip they had learned in town between the two of them after the girls had gone to bed for the night.

Just as Papa entered the edge of the yard, he discovered some newly turned-up earth that appeared as though something might be buried there. Scraping the dirt back with his boot, he found some baked cookies covered up and partly absorbed by the moisture in the dirt. "Who buried these cookies?" Papa asked himself. "I'll see about that when I get back to the house." Papa was going to be late returning to the house to eat supper, but Mama would go ahead and feed the girls early so their food wouldn't get cold.

Saturday evening was the perfect time for Mama to prepare her favorite meal of crisp, fried butter fish she had bought in town. To go along with the fish, she warmed over some field peas and fried some white potatoes with lots of onions in the black iron skillet. Then she made a pan of corn-bread patties and fried them on top of the stove. The girls, by this time, had gotten their appetites back after smelling the delicious fish frying on top of the stove. Before long, they sat down to eat.

The older sisters heaped their plates with fish, field peas, fried potatoes, and a cornbread patty cake with lots of butter melting on top. Before they started to eat, Mama made them fold their hands while she led grace at the table. Ginger and Greta were told to help Nita and Gaye pick bones from the fish before they started eating them so they wouldn't get trapped in their throats. Mama sat Brownese on her lap and fed her off the plate she was eating from.

No one said a word while they were eating, but the girls knew that Mama and Papa were going to leave their big talk until after supper. They all gathered around Mama's chair in her bedroom and waited for Papa to finish eating and the dishes to be cleaned up before the girls began to tell what happened while Mama and Papa were away. Everyone listened without interrupting each other as Lola and Mirah shared their stories about what happened during the day. Earlier, they cautioned the younger girls not to say anything for fear they would tell the wrong things; they especially didn't want Mama and Papa to find out they had been up to mischief. After they heard their stories, Mama ran the girls upstairs and off to bed.

Mama and Papa settled down to rehash what they learned in town about who had visited in the area, gone away, gotten married, or passed away. They also mentioned who was in family way, but the girls were so slow moving upstairs to bed that Mama told them to "scat" before she and Papa began to talk. The girls were still creeping along until Mama said once more, "get upstairs before you get spanked." The girls hung onto every word Mama and Papa were saying, though, until they inched further and further away from the room and could barely hear Mama and Papa's voices in the distance.

Lola knew that this gossip was between Mama and Papa and not intended for the girls to hear. She had heard little bits and pieces of what Mama and Papa were saying, so she knew they had a story to tell, and she wanted to hear it. Lola had a way of sneaking back to the room when Mama and Papa were discussing something they didn't want the younger girls to hear.

Lola waited patiently until everyone upstairs got quiet before making her move. Then she eased downstairs and crept past the front room. She tip-toed and crawled on both hands and knees until she was close enough to stoop near the door to Mama and Papa's room. She was pleased the door wouldn't shut completely because a little crack would let her hear more clearly what Mama and Papa were talking about. If the girls awoke and caught Lola snooping at the door, she would share any gossip she had heard Mama and Papa talking about to keep them from telling on her.

Lola couldn't hear what Mama and Papa were saying unless she strained her ears. She picked up bits and pieces about someone being "turned out of church." She quickly recalled that Mama had warned us teenage girls about how it was custom-ary for the church to drop from the membership roll young women who were in family way out of wed-lock. Lola learned that if the young woman came before the church board and begged forgiveness for committing the sin of getting pregnant before marriage, she might be spared. But if she did not appear before the church board, it would act upon the situation and expel her from church membership. Then she would have to come back to the church with her baby or young child, beg forgiveness for getting pregnant out of wedlock, and ask to be reinstated on the church roll. Again the church would vote on rejecting or accepting her plea.

What ran through Lola's head was the whereabouts of the young man who, no doubt, had been with this young lady before such a sin could possibly have been committed. "Why didn't he just marry the young lady?" Lola asked herself. As Lola continued to listen, she learned that one of Mirah's friends, Rena, had been seen in the company of a young man who was visiting her brothers from over in the next county. He only visited for a week, and sure enough, after about five months, Rena discovered she was in family way. Not knowing what to do, Rena's parents decided that their daughter should get rid of her baby, even though her pregnancy was quite obvious by now. She had begun to fill out in the hips and stomach—everyone who stared at her stomach knew the young lady was going to have a baby.

Rena disappeared from home and went to stay with her older sister up north for a week or two. When she returned home, she had slimmed down and no longer appeared to be pregnant. Everyone simply thought that she had gotten rid of her baby, but no one could prove it.

The church members took matters into their own hands, especially the church board president, Mr. Frigs. He called a meeting of the board to tell how he had been closely watching Rena, speaking with her mama, and had come to the conclusion that she, indeed, had been pregnant. He would ask the church board to vote to expel Rena from the church membership. If Rena had gotten married, she wouldn't have to face the church board, but the young man's whereabouts were unknown. If the child had been born without knowing who the father was, Rena still would be scorned and made fun of because of her bastard child.

Hearing this, Lola sneaked back upstairs, completely stunned by the story Mama had just told. She went to her room and fell across her bed, sobbing alone in the dark, too ashamed for anyone to know what she had just heard. Rena and Mirah were such close friends, and her heart skipped a beat as she thought about how she was ever going to get up enough nerve to tell Mirah what she had heard Mama and Papa talking about.

The church board had its way. The next Saturday, Mama attended the church board meeting. She wanted the elder to pardon young Rena, for she could feel the scorn and hate that could easily come over Rena. Besides, Mama had seven girls of her own, and getting pregnant out of wedlock could happen to any one of them. But Mama's voice was very tiny among all the other negative Christians. She would be the one to talk to Rena's mama and papa, since she was secretary of the church board. Mama hated to tell Rena's parents that their young daughter had been dropped from church membership because she had been in family way and gotten rid of her baby.

The more Mama thought about it, the more she hated doing this task. She wept and prayed long hours with Rena's parents. After this period of prayer, Rena's parents told Mama that Rena wanted to ask forgiveness from the church.

Mama knew this was devastating for Rena's family, but there was nothing she could do to avoid this ugliness. She struggled long and hard over why she had been asked to do such a thankless job, especially since Rena's Mama was Miss Dillah, who had stolen her pocketbook at the fair. That day Mama told Miss Dillah that she would never have any more use for her, but this incident with her daughter proved her wrong. Mama had long since forgiven Miss Dillah for stealing her pocketbook at the fair. Today, Miss Dillah was paying for the sin she committed when she stole Mama's pocketbook as well as the sin her daughter Rena committed when she aborted her baby.

IV. SNATCH THE THORNS

Work on the farm came to a standstill during long hard winters. Papa and Ed sawed and split up a pile of wood and kindling for the stove and fireplace. After the wood was cut, they piled it in a corner of the yard close to the house and bragged about who could chop the most wood. When snow comes, the wood will be within easy reach to keep the fires ablaze in the cook stove, pot-bellied stove, and fireplace in Mama and Papa's room.

Snow kept most of the family homebound, but not without a pot of hot vegetable soup simmering on the stove at least once a week. If anyone went outside the house, it was after the snow had been shoveled and melted along the path out back from the house to the woodpile, outhouse, and barn.

During the winter was also time for peanuts to be shelled that were needed for planting. Papa had hardly any seed peanuts because he sold them for the money to pay bills. He borrowed money from a loan company to buy more seed peanuts for the spring planting. The shelled peanuts cost more than those in the hull, so Papa bought five bush-els in the hull. These had to be shelled, bagged, and made ready for spring planting. The women all joined in for the shelling, especially during the snowy winter weather when the path from the house leading to the road and to the school house was deep with snow.

The younger girls stayed busy cooking and making snow cream—when Mama wasn't look-ing. She never let the girls waste the sugar she needed to sweeten coffee for Papa and to make dried apple puffs for dinner.

Trapping the snowbirds was a weird game for Ginger and Greta. They found a flat board and propped it up in the snow with a short stick. A string that went through the window to the inside of the house was tied to the stick. Bread crumbs were scattered underneath the trap to lure the snow birds to eat the crumbs. As soon as a snowbird appeared and started eating the crumbs, Ginger pulled the string attached to the flat board and trapped the snowbird. If she caught the snowbird, the feathers were plucked and the legs cut off. Then she rammed a piece of wire through the thick part of the bird's legs and singed it over the hot flames in the fireplace. Ginger and Greta teased the younger girls and wanted them to eat the snowbird legs, but they all ran off and hid because they were afraid to eat it. Mama warned them, too, about trapping the snowbirds.

The house had to be kept warm and comfortable, too, and Papa made sure no cracks or crevices let in the cold winter air. Mama complained that the house was old and falling apart. Surely Papa would build them a new one next spring. Whenever Mama spoke to Papa about the drafty cold house, he became disgruntled and hoped she would leave the talk about a new house alone. Papa had more than once told Mama that there was no money to build a house, at least not for two or three years from now, when he hoped the crops would bring a higher yield. For now, they would have to make out with the one they were living in.

It was difficult for Mama to go to the mailbox and collect the mail when snow was on the ground, but she knew it was time for a letter to arrive from Van. It had been over two years since he left, and no word had ever come letting his family know where the army had sent him to serve his duty. Whenever she went to town and saw a man dressed in an army uniform, she walked straight up to him and asked, "Have you seen my son?" She had been told the same story more than once: "Your son left home to go to the war and no one knows exactly where he is." Mama just waited and waited, hoping a letter would arrive any day.

When the roads had been cleared of the snow, the whole neighborhood came awake and started moving about. Papa and Ed used the excuse of clearing the path to the road so they could go back and forth to the store for kerosene and to church on Sunday. Papa and Ed went to town more frequently now, trying to catch up on the local news and to find out what was happening with the war. The real reason the snow was shoveled was because Papa and Ed could stay gone all day. When they returned from town, Papa had loaded the wagon with beans, sugar, flour, salt fish, kerosene for the lamp, and other small supplies, which he got on credit at the corner market in town. He could not bear to return home without bringing something to eat for Mama and the girls.

Before he reached home, he stopped by old lady Girder, who lived alone through the woods from Papa's house, to drop off some flour and beans. While he was there, Papa and Ed chopped a big pile of stove wood so she could cook and keep herself warm while the snow melted. Mrs. Girder had stayed indoors most of the week. Today, she barely stuck her head out the door and said,

"Thank you," Mr. Doll, for cutting the wood. I sure appreciate your kindness."

"You are much obliged," Papa answered. He waved good-bye to her and hopped into the wagon beside Ed, who already had the reins in his hands. Grabbing them from him, he signaled the mules, "Gee!" They took the wagon along a narrow path through the woods that led them home.

When they reached the clearing in sight of the house, they spotted a figure moving swiftly down the path toward the house. Papa brought Lucy and Ginny to a full trot and overtook what appeared to be a man walking with an overcoat fastened tightly around his neck. He wore a black cap tilted to one side, half-covering his face and the entire crown of his head. "Hold up there," Papa yelled at the man. "Who are you and where do you think you're going?" The man whirled around and faced Papa and Ed, who sat there in the buckboard staring in the man's face.

"I'm Russ, your son," the man answered. "Don't you even remember me?"

"No," Papa said. "You left home just a young boy, no more than sixteen." Papa's face lit up when he told Russ that it had been eight years ago since he left home and was all grown up now. "Jump in the wagon," Papa said, "and let me give you a ride to the house." Papa knew that Mama and the girls would be glad to see Russ and welcome his return. "We're glad to have you back, Son," he affirmed.

"It has been a long walk, Papa," Russ reported. "There was no way I could get home from town without walking, and nobody wanted to give me a ride."

"That's okay, Son," Papa assured him. "Go on in the house." Papa told Russ that he has a hot meal and warm bed waiting for him any time he comes home. Ed and Russ picked up the food supplies Papa bought and jumped from the wagon. Papa drove Lucy and Ginny straight to the barn and unhitched them from the wagon. He made sure that they had plenty of fodder to eat and water to drink before they rested after the long trot from town.

No sooner had Ed reached the steps than he flung the door open and yelled, "Mama, Russ is home."

"Who is home?" Mama asked, her eyes popping wide open. As soon as she saw Russ, her arms clasped him tightly around his shoulders and hugged him for at lest five minutes, crying all the while. "You've come back home, Mama announced. "How glad I am to see you."

"I'm glad to be home, Mama," Russ replied, trembling and crying at the same time. "Ten years away has been nothing but hard work, and I didn't have a chance to write or come home."

"But you never let us hear from you. Now that you have come home, I can finally be at peace," Mama remarked. "Where are your clothes?" she asked. "We're proud you came back, Russ, and we welcome you home."

Looking at Russ standing there, he seemed so pitiful and hungry that he didn't know what to say. All those years he was away he never even tried to contact Mama and Papa or to find out how they were doing. Now that he was home, he felt so sorrowful that he hardly could hold back the tears that welled in his eyes.

"Sit down by the fire, Son, and get some rest," Papa begged. "You walked a long ways before you got here. When did you start out for home, anyway?"

"I left two weeks ago." Russ explained. "Some days I only traveled about twenty-five miles, but I made it anyway." Russ told Mama that he was very hungry and asked her to fix something to eat for him. "I waited too long to get back home to eat your good cooking," Russ told Mama. "No one cared for me the way you used to, Mama." She spread out some ham, biscuits, and potatoes for him to eat.

"This is leftover from dinner. Tomorrow I'll cook a special dinner for you to welcome you home," Mama said. After Russ finished eating, Papa took him to the bedroom and stoked the logs heaped in the fireplace. The fire sent bright red flames shooting straight up the chimney, and its bright glow spread warmth all over the room. Papa wanted to know all about Russ's work in the coal mines and how much he got paid. From the looks of him, Papa could tell that he was a distraught young man, certainly with the scars of a hard laborer.

Russ shared with Papa the dreadful life of a coal miner. He began work just a few days after arriving in West Virginia. Some days they stayed in the coal mines all night, working without food or water. When daylight came, they could hardly adjust their eyes to the light, and no sooner had they than they were back down into the mines again. This kept up for years. Russ told Papa that he stayed on the job in the mines because he hoped working conditions would get better. Russ kept hoping and wishing that he could make a living or at least an earning that would feed and clothe him. But it never happened.

Russ told Mama and Papa that Hugh learned better and left the mines over two years ago. You had no way of knowing that Hugh had gone to a big city on the eastern shore and was working in the shipyard, Mama. I heard from Hugh once, and that was the only time.

Russ was sure to tell Mama and Papa that within a few days, he would be moving along, but he wanted to see them first. "I will need a job, and I hope Hugh can help me find one in the shipyard," he explained to Papa. Russ assured Papa that as soon as he can save up enough money, he will send a little home to help out with the farm.

"How will you get there?" Mama asked, softly sobbing. "I don't want to lose you again, Son," Mama complained. "Your stay is so short that I hardly know who you are." She wanted Russ to help them with the work on the farm and assured him that there is a good job at home helping his Papa plow the field if he wants to work.

Mama knew that they could feed Russ well, but they couldn't pay him anything in wages. "Van has been drafted into the army, so we sure do need more help around here," Mama pleaded. Russ knew he would turn down that hard labor offer working in the hot sun as he listened to Mama and Papa talk about Van going to the army.

"If I don't get a job," Russ said, "I'll surely get drafted into the army."

"It's your choice, Son." Mama agreed.

Seeing that Mama had stretched out across the bed to rest and gone to sleep for the night, Russ got up from his chair in front of the flickering embers in the fireplace, said goodnight to Papa, and went upstairs to bed. He lay quietly between the cold, crispy white sheets that Mama had changed on the bed for him. It was the first time since Russ left home that he had slept underneath a sheet. His bed in the mines had been on bunkers, and the men lay stacked in them atop each other fully clothed, awaiting the daylight to bring some degree of comfort. Some of the men got sick, often with pneumonia or tuberculosis, and they coughed throughout the night. Others just lay there, staring at the stars as they shone brightly through the wide-open cracks above their heads. Having found comfort at home, Russ dozed off to sleep.

Russ stayed home for two or three days. After asking about his old friends and killing time playing with his younger sisters, he and Papa walked to the pigpen and barnyard so Papa could show him the fine hogs and cattle he had raised. It was very hard to show Russ the farmlands because the snow was just beginning to melt, and the grounds could barely be seen. He could tell that Papa was very proud of his farm animals. Papa and Russ walked slowly, talking and laughing about the time when Russ was a young lad in school and practiced baseball on a makeshift lot next to the house. Russ was the best ballplayer among all the other boys in the area. His friends had all left the farm life now, and were living scattered about in various cities.

After breakfast a few mornings later, Russ left home, walking toward the road to visit some people he had met in town. As he headed up the path, a man in a black car stopped to give him a lift into town. The man promised to help him find a job, but once Russ got to town, there was no one there to help him. At first he slept in night houses and even without shelter until he could find a job. It took a long time and lots of hard work before he ever got any wages.

Russ never came back home from town that day. Some of Van's friends told Papa that he had gone to the eastern shore and was working in the shipyard. The demand for ships during the war was high, but wages were poor for the men who put in long hours on the docks. Later that year, Mama got a letter from Hugh explaining that Russ was with him and doing well. He had gotten a good job and would be staying with him until he found a place of his own. Hugh promised Mama and Papa that he would try to come home within a month or two to see them and explain why he had left the coal mines and gone to the city.

It took many months before Russ could save money and spend less; and if he did, maybe, yes, maybe, he could help out a little with the farm. But the years went by and Mama and Papa's hope for any speck of income from their sons quickly expelled itself. The only hope and faith they clung

to were their ability to work the farm with the help
the girls gave them.

Spring in the country slowly pushed the winter aside, bringing new hopes, fears, and dreams.
Mirah had started spending many days out of high
school to help on the farm, and she often complained that she wasn't learning anything and didn't
have the money to get the books she needed to
study with. For Lola, it meant riding the school bus
into town alone for most of her high school senior
year, graduating from high school, and finally leaving her home on the farm for somewhere in a big
city up north. She could hardly wait for her last day
of school, so she threw herself into studying and
cramming her brain with all the knowledge she
could get from reading and studying, and waited
for graduation to arrive. Lola knew, though, that
she was somebody special because she would
be the first one in her family to graduate from high
school.

Mama and Papa did not have the one dollar
Lola needed to pay for a rental cap and gown for

graduation, so one of her teachers, Mrs. Bancourt, rented them for her. No one would notice how poor she was, but she was very proud to graduate from high school. Mama and Papa did not attend Lola's graduation. They drove her to town on the wagon the day before and left Lola to stay with Mrs. Bancourt until the graduation ceremonies were over.

Staying away from home was a happy time for Lola because she could frolic with all her friends and listen to what their plans were after graduation: Patsy was going to the industrial college to learn sewing; Johnny was going into the army; Daisy was staying at home to work on the farm; and Tina was becoming a hairdresser. These all sounded like good ideas to Lola, except she knew that she wasn't staying on the farm after graduation.

The night before graduation, Mrs. Bancourt spoke to her about several options she had. None of them sounded right for Lola, but she had to choose something to do in life. She didn't want to stay at home on the farm, so she accepted the offer to work as a live-in maid in New York City. It would take her far away from home at a very young age, but Mrs. Bancourt promised Mama and Papa she would keep in touch with Lola and let them know how Lola was getting along.

Mrs. Bancourt had her plans all laid out for the white family to arrive from New York and take Lola back with them. She even told Lola what clothes to take with her and helped her pack them in an old wooden trunk she drug downstairs from the attic. Mama sewed dresses for Lola and made sure she had ample slips, bras, and panties packed that would last for a year. By then, she would have gotten paid and could shop for her own clothes.

Lola didn't get any time at all for herself. Her job as maid kept her busy, and she had no extra time at the end of the week. She spent most days waiting on her white family from sunup to sundown: babysitting, cooking, cleaning, washing and ironing clothes. Each day after Lola finished working, her mind drifted back home to wonder about her own family, but she didn't think about chopping cotton and peanuts during the hot summer months, robbing her of the fun she never got.

Lola wrote a letter to Mama, and Mama answered it promptly. It saddened Lola to hear the same talk she had gotten before leaving home about sending Mama some money to help out with the expenses for the family. What few pennies Lola was able to save was needed to buy toilet items. She hadn't forgotten about sending money home to Mama; she just didn't have any to send. Soon after she received the letter from Mama asking her for money, Lola started to save fifty cents a week. She wrote Mama that she was trying to make enough money to send for Mirah, and she would help find her a job in New York City. She knew Mirah could get work and help provide herself a living. Together they could scrape up enough money to send some home to Mama for more income to help care for the younger sisters. When Mama broke the news to Mirah that Lola could find her a job, she was very excited about joining Lola in New York and working on her own. Mirah hadn't finished high school, but she didn't care. She couldn't make money going to school, so she was anxious to leave and get away from the drudgery of farm work. She liked the idea of sending Mama some money, and thought that living in the big city was well worth the excitement she felt. At the end of the month, she left home and boarded the Greyhound bus to New York City.

Mirah found a job with a white family in a small town near where Lola worked. She wouldn't be seeing Lola as much as she wanted to, and it caused them to drift apart and live separate lives. The news in the letters Mirah got from Mama kept her aware of how the family was getting along, but Mirah never stopped trying to find out where Lola was. She lived closer to Lola than Mama did; yet Mirah welcomed any little news she could get about Lola.

It was lonely in the different towns where the women worked. They knew very few people and had no relatives who lived in the area that they knew of. Her white family did not associate with

Negroes, and Mirah was not used to being around whites.

By the time summer had gone and fall was upon them, Lola and Mirah were pleased that they hadn't been working in the fields hoeing cotton and peanuts. They knew that Ginger, Greta, Gaye, and Nita would help Mama and Papa with the chopping, so it was never at a standstill. Brownese was barely four years old, but Nita and Gaye were big girls now, so they could easily do the farm work and help Mama out in the house, too. Mama and Papa spent the hardest years of their lives working to make a living after the young women started leaving home.

Ginger and Greta both did the hard work, and Ginger, especially, often filled in to help Papa plow the fields when a spell of rain overtook the crops and caused the grass to grow rapidly. Ginger could plow a clean, straight row that stood up to any row that Papa had ever plowed. Mama fussed with Papa about making Ginger plow, but Papa paid no attention to what she was saying. He just kept her plowing for pretty near the whole summer. Ginger was proud of her plowing, and Papa bragged about it, too. Greta wanted to plow the fields, also, but Papa felt she was not strong enough, and he did not trust her to keep the plow under control. Once when Greta had been trying to plow the garden, she took her attention off the plow and let it uproot a half row of full-grown tomato plants before she could get the mule to stop. After that frightening incident, Papa put his foot down and said that he would never let her touch a plow again.

Everybody on the farm waited for springtime to arrive. The weather cleared up and flowers began to bloom. Mama always planted her garden in the spring, so she anxiously waited for Papa and Ed to start plowing the soil that grew thirsty over the winter waiting for spring rains and fertilizer to start the seeds growing. After they had lain there for a while, the seeds burst through the ground and sprang up to meet the gentle spring rain.

Spring was the time when girls walked to school, held hands with boys, and picked flowers for their mama. Recess at school was a fun time that brought on the start of playing tag, singing "Ring around the Roses," and secret boy and girl talk. Nita and Gaye were best of friends at school. They shared all the stories they heard at school about the boys and the girls they liked. Gaye was a little timid and hid her face every time a boy said "hi" to Nita.

Miss Dale was their new teacher and always a friend, too; sometimes a friend to their Mama as well. Miss Dale kept the girls in line and did special favors and treats for them that she never let the boys know about, and the boys were jealous of that. They told the girls that they were special teacher's pets, but wouldn't dare let Miss Dale know they had breathed a word.

One day at recess, Miss Dale asked Nita and her friend Allie to stay inside during recess because she wanted to talk to them. Nita became shocked and turned to look at Allie to see if she had a surprised look on her face. Her face told Nita nothing. The nearer the time came for recess, the larger

Nita's eyes grew. She became so frightened that she asked to go outside fifteen minutes before recess. She wanted time to relax and think more clearly about what on earth Miss Dale wanted with her and Allie. Rumors flew around the school all the time, but Nita could not remember any rumors about anything she had said to hurt anyone, except for mischievous "girl talk" with Gaye and the other girls that walked home from school on the same route Nita and Allie used.

Nita got back to the room just in time for school dismissal. She stood by the door and watched the rushing students fly past while she twisted her plaits and smiled at each one. When the last student had cleared the schoolyard, she eased herself toward Miss Dale's desk and stood there glaring into her face. Allie stood beside her, pulling at the cute pink sash that encircled her waist.

"You two girls have been the smartest in school this year and have won all the spelling bees that we had," Miss Dale announced. "As always, I treat the two top winners each year, so this year I have chosen you two girls." Allie and Nita stood there stunned. Gradually, Nita let her shoulders droop as she dangled her arms on each side, waiting for the surprise. "You will have to ask your mama if I can take you with me to the picture show," she told Nita and Allie.

"Oh yes!" They both shouted anxiously back to her, without even knowing what picture show Miss Dale was talking about.

"You will have plenty of time to get yourselves ready, but I have already decided to take you two girls to see a Shirley Temple picture show, with Bo Jangles dancing in it," Miss Dale explained. Nita had heard of Shirley Temple, but what she remembered most was the rage throughout the countryside with all the girls trying to sing Shirley Temple tunes and to imitate the way she talked and wore her hair in Shirley Temple curls. Nita and Allie leaped into the air and hugged each other about their big surprise. Nita trotted home as fast as her legs could carry her to ask Mama if she could go to the picture show.

Nita refused to tell Gaye what the surprise was that Miss Dale had told her and Allie, so Gaye had to wait until she got home, running all the way to keep up with Nita. When Nita arrived home, she hardly took the time to put her books down before she burst out the door, with Gaye still trying to keep up, and ran outside where Mama was planting seeds in the garden. "Mama, Mama!" Nita yelled. "Miss Dale is taking me and Allie to see a Shirley Temple picture show."

"When will you go?" Mama asked.

"Mama, why can't I go?" Gaye begged. Mama explained to Gaye impatiently that she was much too young to go to the movie with the older girls. Hearing this, Gaye fell on the ground, rolled over and over, kicked up dust, and went into the loudest screaming and crying Mama had ever heard from her. Gaye could not even think about Nita going to the picture show without her sister tagging along. Mama's word was final. Gaye definitely would not be going to the picture show with Nita.

The next day Mama decided what kind of pretty dress to sew for Nita to wear to the picture show. Never mind that she didn't know when Nita was going to see the Shirley Temple picture show, but she knew Nita would be getting a new dress with socks to match; she wanted her girl to look as pretty as Shirley Temple. Nita tried to act like Shirley Temple, prancing around, singing and dancing, and swinging her dress by the tail. Many times she fell when her feet slipped from under her and when she tried to crisscross her legs. No matter how hard she fell trying to dance to the Shirley Temple jingle, Nita got up. Each time when she tried harder, she fell again and again, until she got all the steps right.

When Nita went to school the next day, the whole playground gathered around her and Allie to hear the gossip about going to see Shirley Temple play in the picture show. They were the stars of the whole school, and they put on enough "airs" to make even the most doubtful believer think that this event was a fairy tale come true.

During class time, Nita and Allie worked as hard as they could on their schoolwork and tried not to get into trouble on the playground. Miss Dale told them that the least little trouble or bad news from either one of them will cancel the trip, and she will take someone else in their place. Nita knew better than to raise any problems, so she threw herself into her school assignments. At home, she dared not to say one sassy word to Mama or even to have anyone else mention her name about misbehaving. If she was being hateful, or picking on Gaye and Brownese, Mama would cancel the trip instantly.

Nita and Allie stayed after school for a few minutes so Miss Dale could tell them more about the trip to see Shirley Temple in the picture show. They needed their ticket fare to the picture show and new patent leather shoes—Miss Dale made sure the girls were not going barefoot. They were to wear cute dresses with crinoline slips underneath them, and a wide sash that tied to make a big bow in the back. Miss Dale would purchase them identical straw hats with ribbons that tied into a bow underneath the chin. She offered to help fix up these two cute girls, and promised them that they would look just like Shirley Temple.

Miss Dale told Nita and Allie they would be leaving school a half day early the day they were going to the picture show. They felt like they were already becoming two very special and precious girls, which made all the other children jealous of them. After talking with Miss Dale, Nita and Allie left school that day, skipping to a Shirley Temple tune she sang in one of the picture shows. They were not sure of all the words to the song, but they knew the tune and filled in some words as they skipped down the path and out of sight of the school house.

When Nita told Mama what she was going to need for the trip to the picture show and when they would be going, Mama cautioned her, "You will have a whole month to get ready, so you'd better behave yourself." "Also," she said, I want Ginger to wrap your hair tonight in small plaits so it will grow into long pretty Shirley Temple curls." Hardly a day

226

went past that Mama wasn't doing something to get Nita ready for her exciting trip. Each day when Nita came home from school, Mama tried something on her that she was sewing. After trying on her new dress once so Mama could fit it, Mama took the dress off of Nita and tried it on again and again. Her crinoline slip had to be made, too, but Mama made the dress first of all so she could lay it aside until Nita was ready to wear it. She was thankful, though, that she didn't have to buy an already-made new dress for Nita. She always kept yard goods on hand in case the girls needed dresses immediately.

Mama was going to town within a week, and taking Nita with her, to purchase shoes and socks. She dared not buy shoes that were fitting too tight, for fear they would be too small for Nita before the school year was over. Mama wanted the socks to match up perfectly with Nita's new dress and needed to take a piece of material with her to make sure. Mama hated buying new shoes and a dress for Nita, especially since she was not able to buy the other girls outfits, too. "Nita is going some-where special," she told the other girls. They stood idly around Mama as she made a fuss over how pretty Nita was going to look in her new dress and shoes.

The day Nita went to the picture show, she came home at lunchtime from school to stay the afternoon. Mama asked Ginger to fix Nita's hair in Shirley Temple curls that would dangle on her shoulders when she walked. First Ginger had to unwind each tiny plait of twisted white string she had wound on each one. Next Ginger washed Nita's hair with a new cake of Ivory soap Mama bought and set Nita out in the sunshine and spring breeze until her hair dried. After her hair dried, Ginger parted it carefully and applied pomade on the scalp and hair. Then she parted the hair again and pressed each piece with a pressing comb she heated on the cook stove top underneath the iron Mama used for ironing dresses and shirts.

It took a long time to get Shirley Temple curls in Nita's hair, especially since Nita liked to squirm around while her hair got pressed and curled. Ginger told her not to move her head because she was afraid that her hand would slip and burn Nita's scalp or the side of her face and leave an ugly brown spot. Moving her head the slightest bit to watch who was coming through the door, Ginger yanked Nita's head back in place so hard that Nita was afraid to even breathe. She didn't mind, though, when Ginger yanked her head over and over to remind her to sit up straight in the chair because she wanted her hair to look pretty.

Ginger knew the curls would last longer if she waited about half an hour to let Nita's hair cool off from the hot straightening comb and let it set about an hour before attempting to curl it with those big black curling irons Ginger clicked in her hand. Even after she curled Nita's hair, she was ordered not to comb her hair or touch her head until Mama had put the dress on her that she was going to wear to the picture show. Although Nita was wearing a new straw hat atop her head, she was constantly told not to touch her hair. If Ginger caught her feeling her curls, she whacked Nita's fingers so hard with the comb that she whimpered, "I won't do it again." She ran to Mama for shelter away from Ginger's cruel hands.

When it was time for Nita to get dressed, Mama laid the clothes on the bed and took Nita into her bedroom so she could start putting them on her, even her new shoes. One by one, Mama pushed the other girls out of the room and closed the door tightly behind them. There was not to be any interruption while she dressed Nita, for fear something would go wrong. She sat Nita in a chair and put her socks and shoes on. Then she stood her up in front of the mirror and put on her panties, underskirt, and crinoline slip. Mama tied a cloth around Nita's head so she wouldn't disrupt the curls as she pulled the dress down over her head and poked her arms through each sleeve hole. Mama slowly twirled Nita around and around, to see if she looked okay, and tied the sash in a big bow behind her back.

Oh, how the dress stood out around Nita's waist. She was going to be the prettiest girl at the picture show that evening. Mama took the rag off Nita's head carefully, letting each Shirley Temple curl fall where it wanted to. "Ginger said for me not to touch my curls, Mama" Nita said. "Can I touch them now?"

"No!" Mama yelled. "Not before you put on your new straw hat."

While Mama was dressing Nita, the girls all lined up beside the door, waiting for Nita to come out. Their eyes became glued to the door trying to catch a glimpse of Nita, even before Mama finished dressing her. When Mama finally opened the door, their eyes sparkled when they saw a cute little girl in a fancy pink dress, and pretty little patent leather dancing shoes standing before them. Nita made a curtsey to her sisters and edged though the door as if she were a little princess getting ready for a grand ball.

Mr. Vant's black shiny black car turned into the path and came to a stop in Nita's back yard. Miss Dale had borrowed Mr. Vant's car, and she was sitting beside him when he drove into the yard.

Miss Dale gave Mama Nita's straw hat, and Mama put it on Nita head and tied a big bow underneath her chin. Nita stretched her long neck inside the car and found Allie's frail body primped in the back seat, too scared to move. She had on a straw hat like Nita's that fastened underneath her chin. Nita got into the car, careful not to wrinkle her dress and knock her cute straw hat sideways, and sat down quietly beside Allie in the back seat. Off they went down the path and turned at the gate toward town. They waved goodbye to Mama and the girls.

When Nita returned from the picture show that night, everyone had gone to bed except Mama. She stayed up waiting so she could take Nita's clothes off and put them away for her to wear to church. Then, too, Mama wanted to hear the news about the picture show.

"Oh Mama!" Nita said. "It was so much fun. I wish I could go again." "Please, Mama, can you take me?" Nita pleaded.

"You will go again someday, child, when I am able to take you," Mama answered.

She told Mama that the man gave her a record so she could play the Shirley Temple song that she was trying to sing. "Mama, please buy me a gramophone so I can play this record the man at the picture show gave me for a dollar," Nita begged. "Mr. Bo Jangles danced in the show, too," Nita said. "He had on a tall black hat and danced around and around so pretty in his black dancing shoes, white gloves, and holding a stick in his hand," Nita sputtered.

Nita started to prance around so she could show Mama how Mr. Bo Jangles danced, but Mama wouldn't let her and whisked her off to bed. "Go to bed, child, and tell me more in the morning," Mama demanded. Nita knew Saturday would be a big day for her because she would have all her sisters' attention about what she had seen and heard at the Shirley Temple picture show. She hoped that sleep wouldn't erase the memory she had plastered in her mind.

The early morning doorbell chimes awoke Lola. She lay quietly and tried to listen to find out who had entered the house where she was working as a maid. "Who are you?" the white woman asked. "Why have you come here?"

"My sister Lola works here for you, and I would like to see her," Mirah replied.

"Oh, you are Lola's sister," the white lady said. "Come on in, dear; she may be still in bed."

Hearing them talking, Lola ran into the hallway and stretched her mouth wide open when she saw her sister Mirah. "I haven't seen you in such a long time," Mirah remarked.

"I'm so glad to see you," Lola said. "Let's go in my room so we can talk." Mirah followed Lola down the hallway and into the room where she slept.

"How is your work here?" Mirah asked. "My job is similar to yours, but my room is so tiny." She told Lola that there's hardly enough space to get a bed in it. Here you have a bed, chair and dresser. You must be getting good pay, Lola. Ignoring her remarks, Lola asked Mirah why she had come to visit her.

"I got a letter from home," Mirah replied. She told Lola that Mama and Papa said they had to struggle to keep the farm going. This year they had another poor crop and that there was hardly enough to keep them from hunger. Mama asked me to send her money to help out with the expenses. She gave me your address, Lola, and asked me to try to find you. "I hate to admit it, Lola," Mirah said, "but I hardly have enough money to buy a bus ticket home." "My live-in family takes food and lodging out of my pay, and there is nothing left some weeks to even buy a stamp and some writing paper," Mirah declared.

"Is that why you have come here, Mirah?" Lola asked.

"Yes," Mirah replied. "If you could help out, too, Lola, that would at least give Mama and Papa a few more dollars to get by on."

"I have no money," Lola exclaimed. "I'm also trying to save up so I can go home."

Mirah told Lola that Mama and Papa also asked that if we have no money, could one of us come home to work. "I have decided that I will take the money I make this week to get a bus ticket and go home," Mirah said.

"You go ahead then," Lola replied. Lola helped Mirah to understand that she will stay on her job and start saving more so she can send Mama and Papa some money next month. She also decided that if she returns home, it will only be for a short time because she will never chop in the fields again. "Mirah, could you please go home and help out?" Lola asked. "I'll stay here in New York and send as much money home as I can."

It took over a month for Mirah to save enough money to get a bus ticket home. Each time she tried to save money, it seemed something else was needed. Finally, one Monday morning Mirah packed up her few belongings and fixed herself a lunch. There was no money saved to purchase anything to eat, so she made a sandwich that would last her until she got home. Mirah headed downtown to the Greyhound bus depot and bought a ticket home.

When the bus pulled into the station for a rest stop, Mirah wanted to make sure that when she got off the bus, she went to the colored section of the bus station. Bus stations are always crowded with long lines of Negroes traveling back home down south, which made it impossible to get to the bathroom quickly. She hoped the bus driver wouldn't take off without her.

When Mirah returned to the bus to continue her ride home, a tall, fat white man had taken her seat near the back of the bus, where colored people sat. She didn't have the nerve and was afraid to ask this strange white man to move and to tell him that he was sitting in the seat she had already paid for. She just stood quietly over the man in the seat, so scared that she feared she would be put off the bus. "Lord, please don't let this create a scene," Mirah prayed quietly. Fear overcame Mirah when she started thinking that if this bus comes to an abrupt halt, and she gets thrown on the fat man sitting beneath her who took her seat, surely he would try to make her get off this bus and accuse

237

her of hitting him on purpose. She felt choking knots in her throat as she thought about a tragedy about to happen and suffered sharp pangs in her legs because she knew there was nothing she could do but stand up frightened and in misery the rest of the way home.

Swinging and swaying, the bus rounded each curve, and buzzed by tiny towns and huge farms. Each farm they passed had strings of Negro workers shaking peanuts and picking cotton. Little children and grown-ups alike were in uneven lines that were so long they sometimes curved out of sight. It was a familiar sight Mirah was returning to.

The bus ride home had taken all day. Once Mirah arrived in the town nearest her house, she would have to catch a ride home to the country. "How would I do this?" She asked herself. "There is no money to pay for someone to take me." Once Mirah got off the bus, surely someone would come by the bus station and offer to give her a ride; but no one would recognize her, since she hadn't been home for such a long time.

It wasn't until early the next morning when Mirah finally caught a ride home with a farmer who had driven to town in his rickety wagon to purchase a few bags of fertilizer for his crops. Mirah never expected to ride home in a wagon, but she was not too proud to do so. Mainly she just wanted to get home from the long journey to see her mama and papa.

Mama, Papa, Ed, Ginger, and Greta had already gone to the field. Nita and Gaye had gone to school. Brownese played in the field at the end of the cotton rows. She was a little older now and would start first grade next fall. Brownese noticed Mirah approaching, so she started running towards her mama and sisters, who were picking cotton in the middle of the field. "Mama!" She yelled in her babyish voice. "Someone's coming." "Who's that lady, Mama? Is she coming to get me, Mama?" Brownese kept asking. When Mama turned her head to gaze at the figure of a woman at the end of the rows, she could tell by the way she walked that it was Mirah. Seeing it was Mirah for sure, Mama waved her hand to her with joy. Flinging down her cotton bag, she ran to the end of the row to greet Mirah, with Brownese trailing behind her. Mirah dropped her satchel and started running toward Mama. After hugging one another, Mirah picked up her satchel and took off toward the house. Mama didn't go to the field the rest of the afternoon, so she listened to Mirah's hardship stories about being away so long, trying to keep her maid job in the city.

Mirah reached into her bra and pulled out a wad of ten one-dollar bills she'd counted in the restroom at the bus depot when she got off the bus. Laying the one-dollar bills flat out on the table in front of Mama, Mirah counted off five and gave them to her. "Here, Mama," she said. "I didn't make as much money as I thought I would; I hope these five dollars will help out some." Mirah smoothed out her other bills left, folded them again, and returned them to her bra for safe keeping.

"Thank you," Mama said with joyful eyes. Mama told Mirah that she will go to town Saturday and buy a few things for the family. We sure do need money. We have no flour, sugar, or coffee, and I didn't know where our next penny was coming from.

Mirah worked around the house and relieved Mama to go to the fields and work. Somehow she exchanged places with Mama. Ginger and Greta thought that Mirah was too good to work in the field since she had lived in the city. Mirah never got into the routine of farm work again. Maybe she would work a half day here and there, but only if she had been promised pay, and no less than a dollar a day. Every dollar she made she saved. She bought nothing to eat and certainly didn't spend anything on junk.

Lola came home the next year for a short visit. She had grown tired of being a housemaid and did not want to stay in the city. The city was attractive, but she never got the chance to go anywhere. Her job as a maid had been too confining and con-stricting. Lola knew she had to support herself, but she didn't want to work as a maid or as a farmhand in the fields. If she could not find a better job, she would be returning to New York to take the job she had left. After seeing all her sisters gathered around her, and after getting all her hugs and kisses from them, she noticed that Brownese was not at home.

"Mama," Lola exclaimed, "where's Brownese?"

"Miss Susan came by the other day and asked me to let Brownese stay with her for the weekend." Mama replied. "She was only to stay for the weekend and promised me she would bring her home the next week and had no way of getting her home before then," Mama explained. Mama told Lola that they could do more work in the fields if they didn't have to watch Brownese all the time. Hearing this, Lola could not believe that Mama had let her baby sister go to live with some other family. That evening when the girls returned from school, they asked Mama over and over if Brownese had come home. They were getting restless that Mama had let her stay away from home so long.

"Mama," Lola insisted. "Why have our baby sister stayed away this long?" Mama could not answer Lola with a good reason. It was as though she had committed a violent act against Lola, and tears of disbelief welled up in Lola's eyes. Brownese's sisters had complete tenderness of heart for her, and the incident was more than they could overcome. The pain over the days and weeks to come grew intensely, seeing that Brownese was never going to come home again.

Miss Susan, one of Mama's neighbors, wanted to help Mama with the girls, so she persuaded Mama to let her keep Brownese for the weekend and to see if she liked staying with her. Weekends and months came and went before Brownese came home for good.

Brownese missed her sisters and brother, but it seemed such a nice place to be, so she didn't mind staying with Miss Susan. She got a chance to go to town nearly every day. She didn't have to play in the fields and watch her sisters working. She played all day with Miss Susan's grandchildren, who lived in the house next door. Whenever they wanted to shop, they rode to town in a big black car to buy some cute clothes for Brownese.

Brownese was at home with Miss Susan. During the middle of the week, they went to Miss Vant's store to buy candy, popsicles, and cookies. These good times lasted for about a year for Brownese, but when Lola returned home again the next year, this time she would not be going back. She coaxed Mama into letting her and Mirah go to Miss Susan's house and bring their baby sister home.

When Mirah and Lola arrived at Miss Susan's house, she thought they had come to visit her. When they told her that mama asked her to send Brownese home, Miss Susan nearly died. She yelled and screamed and cried so loud that Lola and Mirah were scared to even repeat what they had just said. They stood there shocked at what they were seeing.

It took all day to get Brownese ready to leave for home. All her clothes had to be packed, while Miss Susan complained about the money she had spent feeding her, and buying her nice clothes. Miss Susan also felt that she had ownership of Brownese because she was so good and kind to her.

When Miss Susan stopped crying, screaming, and stomping her feet, Brownese began to do the same thing. "You see," Miss Susan said. "She hates going with you home; she hardly knows who you are." But Miss Susan packed her clothes anyway, seeing that Lola and Mirah were not leaving without Brownese. They piled into her big black car and headed home to Mama's house.

Brownese sisters gathered around her, hugging and kissing her and lifting her high into the air. They hid her from Miss Susan until she left in her car, knowing that Brownese would scream if she saw Miss Susan leaving without her.

Lola and Mirah told Mama how hard it had been trying to bring Brownese home. Mama vowed never to let Brownese leave her sight again. She had nearly been stolen by the gypsies when she was an infant, and now she was about to let her baby get away from her again.

Lola's days and weeks at home were spent looking for work in the city and socializing with her friend Janie, who lived in the town where she had graduated from high school. Janie, too, was looking for work, but they also spent time visiting each other, attending the county fair and entering the 4-H Club cooking and sewing contests that were held during the fair. Lola always entered a dress she had sewn that Mama helped her with; but she did the baking on her own, which was everybody's favorite, a pound cake.

When time came for judging the desserts, the 4-H Club officers picked the young men to judge the cakes the young women baked. This year, the prize winner would be going on a picnic with the fellow who judged her cake a first place winner.

Lola stood there in shock when she heard over the bull horn that she had won first prize for her pound cake. No way was she going to a picnic with that long-legged, tall, skinny boy who picked her cake for first prize. He was ugly, too, and tried to grin as he walked toward her. "You're the Chandler girl, aren't you? He asked. "I'll be by your house to take you to the picnic."

"No you won't!" Lola snapped. "You haven't even asked my mama and papa; besides, what's your name?"

"I'll get around to that when I see you again," he replied, grinning. "Until then, I'll see you Saturday after next."

Lola tried to forget all about the boy the instant he walked away, "How can someone I don't even know pick me up and take me to a picnic?" She patiently asked herself. Lola knew that the boy hadn't even been to her house, and she didn't know his name. "But why did he keep asking me if I was the Chandler girl?" she wondered. "He acted like he already knew me."

She knew that Mama and Papa would not let her go to a picnic with a boy they hadn't even met. Lola relaxed when she realized that the picnic wasn't until a week from now. Somehow she kept thinking that he'll forget her by then and won't remember they had ever met.

Lola anxiously waited to get home after the 4-H Club exhibits to tell Mama what happened, and especially that she had won the cake-baking contest. She was too excited to tell Mama all the details about that skinny tall boy who was supposed to pick her up and take her to the picnic. Mama didn't believe what Lola was saying about a boy taking her to a picnic; but she was excited that Lola had won the cake baking contest. Mama was in no hurry for Lola to have someone call on her, especially since she didn't know the boy's name or who his family was.

Lola was restless all week. She kept wondering if she would see this boy before she went on the picnic with him, which was to be held on the following Saturday. Lola wanted Mama to see him first, because if she didn't, she probably couldn't go with him to the picnic alone, unless Mama and Papa said it was alright. She didn't know whether or not Mama and Papa would like him and whether or not she wanted to "keep company" with the boy. Lola didn't want to think about all that now. It was too much for her, for she had never had a boy come to see her before.

Sunday evening before the picnic was soon enough for Leland to come over to Lola's house and meet her parents. She had been anxiously waiting all week long for him to come to her house and hoped he was as anxious to see her as she was to see him.

Sunday, Lola dressed herself in a new dress and went to church. When she arrived, the church service had started. She stretched her neck and looked around to see who was in the pews and if she saw this boy she met at the 4-H Club exhibits. If she didn't see him, she knew right away he would see her when she walked to the table to leave money in the gilded collection plate. Lola took the chance to show herself off and to let everyone see how fancy her new dress looked on her.

When church was over, she and her friends gathered outside in a little group under the shade of a big oak tree. No sooner had they started to gossip about the week's activities than a group of boys strolled over to them. "Hi, I'm Leland," one of the boys said.

"Oh, yes, I met you last week at the 4-H Club exhibits," Lola said. "Do you live around here?"

"I live over on the next farm from your papa, but I have been away at school all year." Leland replied. "I came here to go to church with my parents because they are having their church revival, but I expect to leave next week."

"How will you take me to the 4-H Club picnic then?" Lola asked.

"Oh, I'll see to that and won't miss taking a pretty girl like you to the picnic," Leland answered. "Is your name Lola?" He asked, grinning.

"Yes," Lola replied. She blushed and turned her head aside and looked at Leland out the corners of her eyes.

"Can I take you home in my new car?" Leland asked.

"Yes," Lola answered, hiding her face behind her church fan. She was swept off her feet when her eyes glanced toward Leland's shiny, black, one-seat Ford car with the rumble seat in the back. Rushing off, Lola answered, "Let me tell Mama you're taking me home, Leland, and I'll meet you in front of the church."

Lola rushed off to find Mama and tell her the news. "Mama, I want you to see Leland," she said. "He's taking me home in his new car today. Can I go, Mama?" Lola asked.

"Of course, child, I'll see him when I get home, so tell him to wait," Mama replied. After about fifteen minutes later, Mama climbed into the wagon with Papa. She told him that a boy who was Lola's friend had taken her home in his car. "Let's hurry home so we can see him before he leaves," Mama remarked. Papa trotted old Lucy and Ginny all the way home.

When Mama and Papa pulled up in the yard, they got out of the wagon and walked around Leland's car, admiring its black glistening color.

They looked up just as Leland stepped out the house to meet them in the yard. "Good evening," he called out to Mama and Papa. "I bought Lola home from church so I could ask you if I can take her to the 4-H Club picnic next Saturday."

"Yes, you can take her." Mama spoke up quickly. "That will be so kind of you."

"My name is Leland Garrett. I live across from your back farm," Leland said.

"You are Mr. Garrett's youngest son, the one away at school, aren't you?" Papa asked.

"Yes," Leland replied. "It's a pleasure to meet you all." "It's getting late; I have to get home to eat supper and help my papa feed the horses," Leland added.

"Good-bye," Papa spoke up. "Do come again to visit us, and give my regards to your family." Papa went into the house, where Mama was, and joined the conversation with Mama and Lola. They were discussing the nice young man who brought Lola home from church.

V. DUSTY ROAD

No one in the family knew exactly what to expect during months to come. Burying herself in her work, Mama began one of her house-cleaning tangents that took time away from all the older women and girls in the household to do their share of the housework. No sooner had they finished the work inside than Mama dragged them into the yard to pick up paper, cardboard boxes, bottles, and other trash that had lodged there far too long. These bursts of sudden ambition to clean up all over the house and yard usually signaled that "company was coming." Mama was also known to foresee money, sickness, and death. Each time

something unsavory happened, she sprang helplessly into erratic patterns of behavior that spurted
out half truths such as "I knew it was going to happen," "I could feel it," or "I told you so." No one ever
recalled her telling them anything of the sort, but
somehow, she was convincing about her illusions
of unsuspected incidents. After cleaning had lasted
over four days, Mama and Papa went into town in
search of items they needed before the weekend.

Papa longed for a car to take Mama to town in,
but he knew that would not happen. He had nearly
gotten killed by a train years ago while crossing
the railroad tracks in an old Ford jalopy he had. It
seemed that the car stalled when it hit the bumpy
tracks. Not being able to restart the car, suddenly
Papa became frightened beyond his senses when
he heard the shrill whistle of the approaching train.
He flung himself from the car minutes before the
train approached and rolled over into the ditch,
leaving the car stranded on the tracks. The train
barely missed Papa, but it tore off the door and

smashed the side of the car, leaving Papa and the car in a total wreck.

Hesitating at the door, Papa walked toward the shed and hitched Lucy and Ginny to the wagon and got it ready to take Mama into town. Pulling Gaye and Brownese by the hand, off they went down the dusty road. Papa stayed with the wagon and kept it safe while Mama and the girls darted in and out the stores. But they stayed so long that Papa decided to look for them. Wandering from store to store, he lost all sense of time as he stopped to chat with friends and bow his head to the white folks.

Shopping was so idle in town for Papa that he sat down on the bench in front of the hardware store, killing time watching people stroll by. If no one was blocking his view, occasionally he gazed into the courtyard of the building across the street. This time, his eyes got stuck on that huge red, white, and blue Uncle Sam poster on the court-yard door that read "The war in Germany has left many Casualties." He jumped to his feet quickly and leaned his head more intently toward what he had just read. He thought about Van and wondered if he was one of those casualties that Uncle Sam was telling everybody about. Anyway, several months had lapsed since Mama heard from Van. Papa's imagination struck fear deep into his soul. Somehow he knew casualty meant that something dreadful had happened to Van.

"Good evening, Doll," a soft voice called. "How's Van? My son Winfield came home from the war last week on furlough." Hearing this, Papa yanked his head toward Miss Merlie, who was staring directly in his face.

"What did you say, Miss Merlie?" Papa's weak voice barely squeaked. His eyes bulged as he trembled and froze to his seat.

"I'll ask Winfield to come over for a visit this week," Miss Merlie said. "I think he has to return to his camp before long." She told Papa that her son mentioned something about a ship that was torpedoed had killed some army men. "I'll be going then, Doll," Miss Merlie said. "Give my love to Corinne and the chirren," she added, waving good-bye.

"Thank you for telling me this news, Miss Merlie," Papa said. "I must get the wagon now," he thought. "Then I will try to find out more about the army letting some of the boys come home." When Papa reached the stable where he left the mules and wagon, he had made up his mind that he wasn't going to even mention to Mama what Miss Merlie told him. He was too shocked at what he had just read on that poster, too, so he was going to keep his thoughts to himself until he was about halfway home and could think more clearly. "How could the news of the army upset me so?" He asked himself. Papa thought the sign that read something about casualties meant that some of the men were being killed and that Van wouldn't be coming home. Papa asked himself, "How can I ever find out?" He hitched up the mules to the wagon and went to the spot where he told Mama and the girls to wait for him.

When he arrived with the wagon hitched to the mules, he saw Mama and the girls standing in front of the five-and-dime store, waiting for him. Papa jumped down from the wagon, and the girls hopped into the wagon, one after the other. After helping Mama into the wagon, Papa jumped into his seat in the buckboard beside Mama and drove away to begin the long trip down the dusty road home. Now he would have ample time to tell Mama the news Miss Merlie had told him.

Mama sat up straight in disbelief and stared into Papa's sunken face when he told her that Winfield had come home on a furlough and what he had just read on the Uncle Sam poster. "I wonder where Van is now." Mama stated. "Certainly if he had been killed in the war, someone would have come to the house and told us."

"Miss Merlie seemed to think that Winfield told her that Van had been overseas but was going to be shipped to the States," Papa stated. "The ship he might have gotten on was hit with a torpedo that wrecked a shipload of army men." Feeling scared that she would never see her son again, tears wet Mama's cheeks. Such rumors do go around, but Mama was too afraid to even think about whether or not Van was alive. She had not heard from him in months. She felt a little sad because when she answered his letter, she joked with Van about ending his letter saying, your "sun" instead of your "son." Mama hoped he didn't take this as an offense, but rather as a joke, and would not be angry with her. Mama never heard from Van again.

Van came home from the war the following week, thankful that he had been spared his life and had escaped the war without being killed. Having traveled by train from out west for nearly ten days, Van arrived in town early one morning and had nearly walked home before a man stopped to give him a ride in his truck. Fearing the sight of his uniform, he dumped Van out just short of reaching home.

He traveled onward down the dusty road toward home, where he had left a few years earlier. He had walked this path before, and with each step Van took, a film of fine dust settled on the bottom of his army trousers and shoes. He didn't mind the dust on his pants because he wouldn't be wearing his uniform after he got home. Nearing home, he noticed that the door on the back porch was falling apart, but he would climb on up anyway and sleep there until daybreak.

Mama, Papa, and the whole household were asleep when Van arrived. He didn't want to awaken them, so he pulled his crumpled army overcoat out of the sack he carried on his back and placed it underneath his head. In no time he was asleep. Had he come home a month later, the bitter, cold night would not have allowed him to sleep there on the porch. It was chilly and frosty during the night, and he shivered from the cold, but he was too tired to even care.

Van's dreams tormented him and wouldn't let him be at peace. Lying there in the chilly comfort of his home on the farm, those horrible dreams kept bringing him memories of the worst days of his life when he was fighting the Germans in the war. They were cruel and frightening days; many of them were times when he barely escaped with his life aboard a ship. His dreams brought dreadful images of the war back to him as clearly as if they were happening all over again. Those piercing, agonizing sirens tore at his nerves and kept scattering his memory of the action over the calm waters again and again. He screamed with terror in his dreams, and they continued to tear him to shreds. These were the times when Van became silent and kept those scary moments to himself. This fury even followed him after he awoke from his dreams. Fear wouldn't let Van breathe a word about these war demons he encountered, which tore at the core of his senses.

There on the porch at home, he felt Papa shaking him to awaken him from his turmoil. "Van, when did you get home?" Papa asked. "Why didn't you awaken us when you came home?" He nudged Van. Too frightened to speak, Van's bulging eyes glared up at Papa. Van rolled over and jumped up on his feet. He shook himself briskly, awakening from the tormenting dream that kept him frozen in fear.

"Is that you, Papa? How—how did I get here?" Van asked. Papa could tell by the scary look on Van's face that he had gone through a few chilling and frightening years because of the war. Papa had heard how it was like in the army, but he never knew it would take such a toll on Van. Van didn't even act like himself.

"I was supposed to go to my next fort assignment," Van explained. "I also wanted to come home, so I went 'over the hill,' Papa." Van kept telling Papa that some army men might come looking for him, and if they did, Van made Papa promise him that he would tell the army he hadn't seen him and didn't know where he was. Van wanted Papa to know that the war was terrible, and that he didn't have any intentions of staying in it.

"There was a scared incident that almost killed me, Papa," Van said. Let me tell you what happened, Papa. "A German U-Boat torpedoed our ship and sliced off the top of it. I was on that ship, Papa, when it was trying to get us home. The top was sliced off as if a blade of some sort had attacked it and left us to perish at sea. Only about fifty of us men on that ship load of army men survived that horrible night. The ship, luckily, after partly floating and drifting on the high sea for long days and nights, was brought ashore in France. Then we were air-shipped to a stateside base out West."

Van complained to Papa that he decided then that he would find his way home the first time he got a chance. The war hadn't ended, but it sure was the end of Van's time in the army, and none too soon. "I'm never going back, Papa. I'd rather stay here on the farm and help you." Van stated boldly. "That's just as good an excuse as any."

Van told Papa that as far out as they live in the country, Uncle Sam will never come looking for one army man. He wanted Papa to know that he was a deserter filled with fear and was through with the army. "I—I'm scared," Papa, Van said.

"We will keep you safe, Son," Papa assured him.

"I hate the army. Besides, those of us who got injured on that ship were taken to the hospital. After they examined us, they said we were 'shell-socked' badly and would never be able to stay in the army. I didn't wait around to find out what they meant by that. I just walked out of the hospital and tried to find my way straight home. It took me a long time to get here, walking part of the way, Van told Papa, but I didn't care."

Papa ran into the kitchen and yelled, "Van's home, everyone. He's here on the porch!"

"Van, when did you get here?" Mama asked, as she flew out of the bedroom and onto the porch, where the family circled around him. Mama pushed her way to Van and looped her arms around him and said, "Welcome home, Son, we're glad you're back." "The war is a horrible thing, Mama said to Van. "Look what it did to you." Releasing her hold on Van, and stepping back to look him over more closely, Mama held her chest and began to sob heavily as her whole body heaved up and down. "Let me fix you something to eat," Mama said.

"Then you get some rest for a few days." Mama shoved the girls out of her way and told Ed to help her take Van's sack of clothes upstairs and set them in the room. Van followed them without saying a word. "Lord have mercy, my son has come back home," Mama mumbled.

Van fell across the bed thinking what he would do with so much time now that army life was behind him. He went to sleep again and was awakened when Mama yelled, "Van, come downstairs to eat your breakfast."

During breakfast everyone at the table was anxious to hear what Van had to say about the army and what had happened to him while he was away. The questions came too fast for Van to answer, and were too confusing when everyone talked at the same time. Van looked confused, too, and muttered some words in a strange tongue. Mama looked at Papa, frowning, and Papa just shook his head. The girls became frightened when they saw Van looking so strange. Van never spoke another word. He just sat there eating as though he was starved. "When was the last time you ate?" Mama asked. Ignoring her, Van never answered Mama's question about the army and his part in it, and no one ever asked him another question about the army. As far as Van was concerned, he had put the war demons in the back of his head; it was over and done with—so he thought. Van was even too frightened to mention the army to anyone. Mama and Papa knew he was shell-shocked, just like the hospital told Van, so they vowed to protect and shield him from his mental army problems.

No one ever approached Van about what he did in the army from that day on. The army men neither came looking for him, nor did they ever find him. Papa was glad for Van that no one ever did. Van was home now, and Lord knows, Papa sure could use another plow hand on the farm because he was getting up in age now and his patience for farm work was waning. In fact, Papa once told Mama that after a few more years of hard work, he wouldn't ask a mule to "git up" if it sat in his lap.

Van was up early Saturday morning. He and Papa went into town to find out if anyone had been looking for him. After inquiring in town about the army, Van searched in the clothing store for a pair of pants and a shirt to wear. He had only army clothes, but he wanted to throw them away. He knew he would need money, but he had none. He would have to hire himself out, but he had to be careful not to let the army or anyone else know he had gone over the hill. Papa had very little money. As usual, he blamed it on the poor crop that year. He was very proud of Van because he had gone to war and returned home. Papa gave Van a few dollars to spend on clothing.

Before returning home, Van wanted to visit some of his old buddies he knew before he left for the army. Where were Johnnie and Bill now? Thinking about them and the many times they had been out together, he and Papa stopped by the local Dew Drop Inn café in search of his hometown friends he hadn't seen in years.

As soon as he reached the door, the men and women in the room rushed toward Van and lifted him off the floor. His buddies welcomed him home with wild hugs. They all bought him liquor to drink, which slowly made Van drunk.

As the night wore on, drunken brawls broke out between several groups. Van and Papa, getting restless now, headed for the door. His buddies thought they were trying to help increase the fighting, so someone in the crowd shot a pistol wildly in the room. One bullet ricocheted off the ceiling and pierced Papa in the leg, and another bullet rammed though Van's right foot.

Too frightened at what had happened to them on Van's first night out, Papa and Van didn't dare go to the hospital because no one was supposed to know that Van had gone over the hill from the army. They went straight home, frightened, hurting, and groaning painfully. They were even more frightened to tell Mama what had happened to them, but they knew she would find out.

"I told you about hanging out at juke joints, Mama said. "Now look at the two of you."

Hearing this, Papa became irritable and yelled, "For God's sake, woman, get some bandages and bathe these wounds."

"Mama, I got shot in my foot, and it left a hole where I got shot, Van said. "One bullet hit Papa in the back of his leg, but it went through his leg." Immediately, Mama found some rags and strapped up their wounds to stop further bleeding. "The wounds would take a while to heal," Mama thought. "Neither one of them would be able to do any work for a week or two."

Van and Papa just sat around the house looking at each other and thinking about how foolish it was of them to go to a place like that. They remained in their seats from morning to night, moving only once or twice to eat their meals. The two of them were much too ashamed to leave the house; they feared someone would ask what was wrong with them and why they had gotten shot. They never returned to that juke joint again.

Van was too frightened to ask for assistance from the army with his psychological problems; however, he was ordered back to school after the war was over. Luckily, the army rewarded him for attendance. After all, he had disappeared, and he didn't want the army to know where he was.

Mama and Papa never questioned Lola about her new beau Leland, so the courting between them continued. Her sisters were talking about how they were getting awfully close and familiar with each other. The courting between Lola and Leland spilled over and extended to every weekend when they went to picture shows during the week, picnics on Saturdays, and church on Sundays. Sometimes they met other couples and rode with them to and from church or the picture shows.

Mama and Papa began to wonder about their daughter's relationship with Leland, also, especially when they started staying out real late on Saturday nights. When Sunday morning rolled around, Lola was always too tired to go to Sunday school and wanted to sleep late. Mama didn't bother her and let her have her way. This didn't last long, though. It bothered Mama that Lola had promised Leland he could pick her up at home and drive her to church in his brand new Ford car every Sunday. No sooner had church started than Lola strolled into church, with Leland right behind her. He sat with the men and Lola found her seat beside Mirah, who secretly promised to save it for her.

Lola never walked to the church again, or rode with Mama and Papa in the wagon. Leland was always around to pick her up, take her to church, and drive her back home, if she went out at all. He showed up week after week at the same time to repeat the churchgoing on Sundays. These trips back and forth to church gave them a chance to see each other and to have long conversations about love and the good times they were having together.

Leland wanted to marry Lola, but they both were scared that their parents would not allow any such action. "I'll have to be brave," Leland thought, because I do really love Lola, and we don't want to live without each other anymore." "Do you mind if I ask your Papa if I can marry you, Lola?" Leland asked.

"Let's try it and see," Lola answered. The following Sunday when Leland brought Lola home from church, he decided to stay there with Lola until her mama and papa arrived home in the wagon. They knew it would be late in the evening, but Lola and Leland sat patiently on the front porch waiting for Mama and Papa to arrive.

No sooner had the mules headed down the path with Mama and Papa sitting primly in the wagon and staring straight ahead than they noticed that a man was sitting on the porch. As the wagon turned to go around the corner of the house, Leland's car came into view. "That's Leland," Mama said. "Why has he decided to bring Lola home and stay here until we arrive?"

"I don't know, but we will soon ask," Papa replied.

Mama and Papa lit down from the wagon and walked straight past the girls, who were not allowed

272

on the front porch when company came. They said "good evening" to Leland, who sat there beside Lola. After they exchanged greetings and began talking about the sermon they had heard at church, Papa struck up a conversation and asked if they liked going to church regularly together.

Shortly thereafter, Leland asked Papa to step down from the porch into the yard and take a little walk with him up the dusty lane because he wanted to discuss something with him. Papa agreed, so the two of them took off toward the cedar tree on the hill at the end of the lane. They stood there underneath the shade and talked for what seemed like an hour. Craning their necks as far as they could hear and see, Mama and all the women, except Lola, were curious about what Leland wanted to talk about. Mama questioned Lola, but she tried not to blush or let on to Mama what Leland was talking to Papa about.

Finally, when everyone had drifted into wild chit-chat about other things, Papa and Leland returned from up the lane under the cedar tree. Leland walked straight to his shiny Ford car without even saying good-bye to Mama or Lola, spun it around, and fled up the path away from the house. "What a weird way to act," Mama said. "Leland has never left here without saying goodbye, but this time he did." Then all eyes gazed at Papa, straining to see the look on his face and to hear what he had to say.

Papa escaped to the barn to feed the mules, cows, and hogs. By the time he finishes, Mama and the girls will have scattered and gone to bed. He was too stunned himself to talk right away, and he needed time to think before he could tell Mama what Leland had talked about under that mystic cedar tree. Mama would hear none of that. Needling Papa, she cajoled and cornered him so sternly that he was forced to tell her what Leland had said to him. "Leland asked me if he could marry Lola," Papa whispered, his voice trembling.

"What?" Mama asked.

"Leland wants to marry Lola, so I guess she told him that it's okay with her," Papa repeated.

Mama knew that Lola had been looking very bright-eyed and anxious whenever Leland came around, but she had no idea that getting married was ever on Lola's mind. Finally, after Mama and Papa had discussed the ins and outs of this upcoming event, Mama wondered how Lola felt about getting married and leaving home. Lola certainly was of age to get married. She had passed her teen years now, and was a young woman. But she was not prepared for what Lola was thinking.

Lola told Mama that she wanted to get married and leave home. She hated the work in the fields, and she wanted more out of life than what she was getting from the day-to-day toiling in the wretched fields under the broiling sun. She convinced Mama that she wanted something better for herself. Hearing this, Mama could only agree with her. She loved Lola with all her heart but had not dreamed that her daughter one day would be taken from her in marriage. Being the first of her young women to marry, just the thought of losing her daughter in marriage to Leland was a little scary. Mama and Papa knew very little about him, except that he came from a respected and well-to-do family who lived on the low-ground road.

Lola was happy and excited about marrying Leland, and Mama was not interfering with her feelings. Mama and Lola discussed her wedding plans each night, and as the weeks went by, Lola was pleased to know that Mama and Papa were glad to give her a wonderful wedding.

Lola planned for the day when she would walk down the aisle to marry Leland and move away from home. She had only a few married friends who lived nearby, so Lola relied heavily upon their advice to help her plan her wedding. Lola and Mama talked about how the wedding dress would look, how much money it would cost, and who would be the maid of honor. It certainly was to be held at the church one Saturday in August, but no special date had been set. The next time she saw Leland, the date would have to be worked out.

After filling Mama in on the plans for her wedding, Mama and Lola went to the dry goods and dress material store to look for wedding dress patterns. Mama was an expert seamstress, so there was never any mention of a store-bought, ready-made wedding dress. They found a pattern Lola liked and bought the white satin for the dress and netting for the veil. Mama tried to pick a simple wedding dress and veil pattern, for she had only a month before the dress was needed. Wedding dresses required exact fittings, so Mama needed time to get it ready.

Lola was at Mama's side while she was making her wedding dress from start to finish. She didn't want to miss an important fitting, and she wanted every stitch the sewing machine made to look just right. Then Mama had all the bridesmaid dresses to make for Marta, Grayce, and Flocie. Mama didn't mind fitting the young women and sewing the dresses at no charge, but there was no money to buy the material for another dress. Lola dreaded asking her bridesmaids to pay for their own dresses, but she had no choice, and she certainly didn't have anyone else to use for bridesmaids—except her sisters. She wanted her baby sister Brownese as flower girl, but she knew Mama would say no because of the money she needed to buy her a dress. Lola's maid of honor, Marta's daughter, was as cute and sweet as Brownese. When Lola asked her maid of honor to dress her daughter for the flower girl, she was too happy to do so. Lola's family brooded for many days over not taking a part in their big sister's wedding. Mama thought that Lola was ashamed of her family and her home because they had no money, and that didn't set right with Mama. She took it to heart, but she told Lola that her family was all she had and that she might need them one day.

Mama was thrown into the wedding day whether or not Lola was ready. Her dress was made of pure satin, which would cascade far behind Lola as she approached the altar. Her veil of thin netting was attached to a headband of tiny pink tea roses and pearls, ready to be draped over her face before going to the altar.

Mama went to church early the fourth Saturday afternoon in August to see that last-minute items and incidentals were neatly arranged and taken care of properly. She took with her the wedding cake, her clothes she would be wearing for the wedding, and the lemonade punch for the reception. Her job was to see that each bridesmaid's dress fitted properly and that their shoes matched each dress. As each bridesmaid entered the church, Mama was there waiting to take them to the dressing room where the bride would change into her wedding gown.

The flower girl was dressed, and her basket of flowers was placed beside her, ready to be strewn down the aisle. She could hardly wait to be seen strewing rose petals down the aisle and was told to sit down constantly.

Mama wanted the wedding to be perfect, so she arranged where each bridesmaid would stand at the altar. Then she turned her attention to Lola, who had already put on her underclothes and was ready to pull the wedding dress over her head.

"Don't mess up my hair," she told Mama, and urged the bridesmaid in front of the mirror to help Mama with the dress. Lola did not want any wrinkles in her dress; also, the train on her gown was to cascade behind her without wrinkles. The tiny little pearl beads and roses around the neck and sleeves of her dress were neatly arrayed and nestled separately in place.

Straining her neck to check whether or not guests had arrived, and if the organist was seated, Mama caught a glimpse of Leland, his best man, and ushers on the far side of the church. She motioned to the ushers to form a line at back of the far right aisle because the wedding will begin in just five minutes. Leland nodded back to Mama; and with his nod, she dashed back into the dressing room, where one of the bridesmaid was smearing the last bit of rouge on Lola's face. She indeed was a stunning girl, and even more beautiful in her wedding dress.

Mama carefully placed the veil over Lola's face, and she fingered it gently, trying to get it to fall in place just right. Lola turned around and placed herself in front of the full-length mirror on the door, admiring how beautiful she looked. Mama placed a delicate pink rose that she plucked from her flower garden on each bridesmaid's dress and asked them to stand in the back of the center aisle and not to move before the wedding march began. They stood there, excited and happy to be walking down the aisle with Lola.

At 5:00 p.m. sharp, the wedding music began. The bridegroom and the best man walked in and stood in front of the altar. Then the maid of honor walked down the aisle and took her place at the altar. Next, the bridesmaids and ushers marched down the aisle and took their places opposite each other at the altar. They all stood there quietly until the organist struck a cord for the bride to march in, and for the audience to stand up and receive the bride coming down the aisle.

With a bouquet of pink roses in one arm and the other one looped around Papa's arm, the bride marched slowly toward the alter. Papa was smiling, and with each step, he showed excitement over the pleasure of giving away his beautiful daughter. As they slowly marched, Papa tightened his grip on Lola's arm when he almost tripped on the carpet.

When the minister began the ceremony, he motioned to Lola and Leland to face each other in front of him. Lola's eyes met Leland's, and as soon as the minister asked who gives this bride away, Papa sighed with relief and uttered loudly, "I do." Then he took his seat in the front-row pew beside Mama.

"Do I look okay to Leland?" Lola wondered. She was somewhat in a trance when the minister ordered the rings to be exchanged, so the maid of honor took the bouquet from Lola's arms, handed her Leland's ring, and held the bouquet until the rings were exchanged on the bride and bridegroom's finger. Immediately after the minister gave Leland permission to kiss the bride, Lola's heart skipped a beat as Leland removed the veil from her face, exposing all her beauty, and placed a passionate kiss on her lips and cheeks. "You look lovely," Leland whispered. He grabbed his bride's arm and walked out the church.

Lola and Leland entered the reception as husband and wife. They made sure to greet the guests and thank them for their support and well wishes. Afterwards, they cut the cake, opened their presents, and gave a toast to the guests. Before leaving the reception, Lola happily flung her bouquet of roses into a crowd of ladies in waiting and left the reception.

After changing from her wedding dress to a beautiful pink suit, Lola met Leland at the door. They hugged and kissed each other as the guest craned their necks trying to get a glimpse of the husband and wife or hear about where they would be honeymooning. With a smile stretched across Lola and Leland's face, they stepped into Leland's car to unknown whereabouts, leaving the wedding party behind.

Lola never spent another night at home. She seemed to forget all about Mama and the rest of her sisters and brothers. She went to live with Leland at his stepmother's house after she returned from her honeymoon. Lola didn't mind moving over to another farm, but she never picked up a hoe again and chopped a row of cotton or peanuts for Papa. Mama saw that she liked her new family and was quite happy for Lola.

Lola and Leland stayed on Leland's farm for a very short time. They never worked on the farm after they married, but they enjoyed going to parties and drinking whisky on weekends. When their finances got low, they moved to live in the city in the projects where Leland bought property and opened a dry-cleaning business. Lola got a job working as a clerk in a grocery store and working in her husband's cleaning business on Saturdays. They were able to make a good living for themselves on the food she got from the store in exchange for the already low wages she was paid. Leland purchased more property and moved out of the projects into a beautiful new brick home.

Mama looked to Lola to send her money to help her with the rest of the girls at home, since she and

Leland were doing well in the city, but she never did. Lola didn't like Mama begging for money, so she became angry and began to hate her family even more because they were so poor. She bought Mama some dresses, hats, pocketbooks, and pretty shoes on credit, but Mama needed money more than anything else. Occasionally, Lola gave her spending money whenever she could spare it. Lola let Mama visit her in the city, bringing Brownese with her, but not very often. She never gave her younger sisters, Ginger and Greta, a chance to visit her in her home in the city; neither did Mirah, Nita, and Gaye visit her. Lola didn't want any of her sisters around her new friends, and she never took her friends to see her sisters and brothers.

Mama just punished herself, always telling the girls that Lola was too busy to think about them. None of her sisters believed what Mama was saying because they could see that Lola didn't like being around her family. She did her best to abandon them, hoping they would go away and hide somewhere so she could just forget about them.

Lola loved to visit Mama on Mother's Day and bring her gifts. Once when she came home, Leland was too drunk to bring her, so she caught the Greyhound bus to the overgrown road to see Mama. She walked through the dusty, cutoff path until she came in sight of the house. As soon as she set foot on the steps, Mama met Lola at the door and told her, with fire in her eyes, that she thought she was a tramp coming down the path toward the house on a Sunday morning. That kind of talk made Lola so angry that she plopped the gift she brought Mama for Mother's Day on the table and left the house half walking and running, smothering curse words beneath her breath as fast as they flared up in her head. She yelled at Mama and told her that she never would walk down that dusty path to see her again.

When Mirah had saved up enough money for bus fare, she left Mama and Papa stranded on the farm and took off to the city where Russ and Hugh were living. The two brothers were glad she had come to live with them, and they helped her to find a room to let in the apartment house where they lived. Mirah was tired living on the farm, working harder than she did when she was hired out as a Maid. She knew it was time for her to leave.

Mirah hated being single and wanted to get married just like Lola. She knew that when she met a man who wanted to marry her, she would say yes as soon as he asked. She wondered how it felt being married and if she would be loved and taken care of like Lola. She started keeping house and living with Nate, a man who was from the Deep South and who came to the city to work in the shipyard. They got along well for a while and later married.

When Mirah's first baby arrived, Mama was very proud of her. She stayed in her own home with her husband and baby, but her jealous husband soon brought strife to their growing family. They fussed and argued about money and bringing up their children. They even struck each other occasionally when they got into heated arguments.

When Mirah got pregnant with her second child, the fighting between her and Nate increased. This time he made her leave home. She had no place to go, so she and her children returned home to stay with Mama and Papa for a while. Mirah had nothing with which to care for her children. She only knew how to clean house, but she could barely save enough for herself. She left her children, Maela and Tony, with Mama and returned to the city to look for work.

At first, she tried to live with Nate without the children, but he continued to treat her mean, so Mirah separated from him for good and later moved out and tried to live on her own. She asked Mama to keep her children much longer than Mama wanted to, but Mirah had no other choice, since it was so hard to find work that would pay her enough to hire a babysitter.

Mirah thought she had settled for good, since she had found a second menial job working in a café. She lived alone for a while, without caring for her children and relying on Mama and Papa to take care of them whenever she was out of work. For a while, everything seemed to go right in the city for Mirah and her brothers, but the wages were poor. They made up for the lack of good jobs with night life, which they enjoyed on the weekends. Mirah and her brothers frequented night spots, drank whisky, and stayed out late on weekends in juke joints where the neon lights invited them to hang out and have some fun.

This kind of living was new to Mirah. When she worked up north for a white family, she was not allowed to go out at night to see the sights. Here in this city, she had no one to tell her what to do or where to go, so she let herself run around to night spots with her brothers. Saturday nights were high times for them; thus, Mirah worked hard during the week and saved her money so she could go out on weekends to juke joints instead of sending it home to Mama, who was caring for her children.

What Mirah was doing in the city quickly became ugly. One day as she was coming home on the bus from her day job, she met a young woman named

Kallie who lived across town. She told Mirah she was new in town and had come to the city to live on her own. She asked Mirah to show her around the town, since Kallie had lived on a farm with her parents until she was nineteen years old and knew nothing about the city. Mirah was more than glad to show Kallie around the town, but first she wanted to introduce the young woman to her brothers. They planned to meet Mirah's brothers, Russ and Hugh, at the Skipper Beer Parlor on Saturday night. Kallie could hardly wait to meet her brothers, but she knew that she had the choice to make about which brother she would pick for her boyfriend. When Saturday night came, Kallie could hardly wait to go out with Mirah. She dressed in her prettiest dancing frock and plastered makeup all over her face so she could look exotic, yet tempting and beautiful to the men.

She and Mirah had been in the beer parlor no longer than ten or fifteen minutes before Hugh and Russ walked through the door. Mirah and Kallie were sitting in a corner booth in the back of the juke joint in deep conversation when Mirah looked up and saw Hugh and Russ standing near the door, looking over the joint. Mirah stood up and waved to them with a bottle of beer in her hand.

"Hello," they each said, one after the other.

"How y'all doing?" Mirah replied. "I want you to meet my friend Kallie."

Russ was pleased at having met Kallie. Mirah could tell because he wouldn't let his eyes tear away from her face. When Mirah and Hugh were ready to leave, Russ offered to take Kallie home in a taxi cab and told Mirah and Hugh that he would leave later. Hearing this, Mirah and Hugh left the beer parlor and went home.

Russ was outgoing and friendly and considered anyone he met a good friend. One night when he took Kallie to a bar down town, Russ hugged and kissed a woman he had met on his job and began talking to her. He had no idea that Kallie was jealous of him, especially since he hardly knew her. But he had taken her out that night, so Kallie felt that Russ should give her all of his attention. When

Kallie asked him about the woman and why he was hugging and kissing her, they started up a heated argument.

Russ and Kallie argued and fought right there in the juke joint where they had gotten drunk. As the argument got worse, Russ started slapping Kallie. She pulled out a tiny pin knife, opened the blade, and stabbed Russ in the neck, severing his jugular vein. At first he was stunned that he had been stabbed. When he fell to the floor, Kallie slipped out into the night, unheard of and unseen to this day.

Drunks in the juke joint panicked looking at Russ lying there, bleeding to death on the floor. They were all in such disbelief at what they were looking at, so no one thought about calling an ambulance to take Russ to the hospital in time to stop the bleeding and to give him a blood transfusion. Russ went into shock, as well as the spectators who were standing over him. Someone in the crowd yelled, "Call an ambulance!" But it was almost too late, for Russ had nearly bled to death. The ambulance driver never tried to revive him. He just rushed him to the hospital, too late to save his life. Russ breathed his last breath and was gone just as the medical attendants stretched his limp body onto the examining gurney.

Early the next morning, Mirah got up and hurried to the Western Union station to send Mama and Papa a telegram that Russ had been killed—stabbed to death by a woman he hardly knew. When the telegram arrived, Mama went into hysterics. She hurried to the field to tell Papa, who unhitched Lucy from the plow and came running to the house with Mama.

"Did Mirah say who did this terrible thing to Russ? Where is he now? and how will the matter be taken care of?" Papa kept asking. "There is no money, and I'm sure I'll have to bury him." Mama said nothing. She just waited to see what Hugh and Mirah would tell them when they arrived home.

Late that night, Mirah sent another telegram to Mama and Papa, saying she would be home with Russ's body and for them to prepare a gravesite at the back gate on the farm, where he would be buried beside his grand mammy and grand pappy. Mama had to let Mirah know what day and time the funeral could be held. The body would be sent to the farm, where Mama and Papa lived. They would make the final arrangements for Russ's burial.

On the day of the funeral, Mama was so hurt that she barely would look at the young girls. She just walked about the house crying and sobbing quietly. She tried to hide the sorrow in her heart, but when each girl saw her sobbing, she asked, "What's wrong, Mama? Are you sick?" Without answering these questions, Mama just hung her head lower and cried more softly. Mama cried for Russ because she felt so hurt and sorry for him. He had been in the city for such a short time, and now he was gone.

Mama kept Nita, Gaye, and Brownese home from school on the day when Russ' funeral was held. Brownese was just entering elementary school the last time Russ came home; she and the other young girls hardly remembered seeing him at all when he was alive. His funeral was sad for the young girls, but it was a lasting memory of their older brother Russ.

"Why are you wearing that black dress and hat, Mama?" Gaye wanted to know. Mama didn't answer her; she just turned her head and continued sobbing softly to herself. After the funeral, the family returned home. The next day they went to the grave site where Russ was buried. They stared long and hard at his gravestone, hoping they could recall some lasting sign of life as he lived it. They knew that the memories of him would be lost forever.

Mirah and Hugh spent the night at home. The next day Papa spoke to them about the city and begged them to stay at home with him. Hugh complained that he had to go to his job the next day. He reached in his pocket and pulled out a ten dollar bill and gave it to Papa. Mirah told Mama she was working for a white lady cleaning her house and asked the woman to hold the job for her until she returned. Mirah told the woman that she had to go home to bury her brother and would surely return within a few days.

Hugh and Mirah both returned to the city to face the bright lights without their brother Russ. Mama hoped that if Mirah was not staying on at home, she was taking her kids with her. That didn't happen, either.

It was so sad for Mirah to leave Russ home in his grave alone on the farm and saying good-bye to her children, Maela and Tony. They were in Mirah's thoughts as she and Hugh drove away, knowing that at times it would be lonely for them in the city without Russ, but they also knew that their lives must go on without him.

VI. KILLERS OF THE HARVEST

Mama believed that Gaye's teenage years would be challenging because she grew up so fast. The tenth grade exposed her to boys in the eleventh grade who often chased after her and begged for easy sex. Besides, they introduced her to beer and whisky and dared her to get drunk with them after school was out until she was ready to catch the school bus back home. Sometimes trashy boys drove by where the school bus stopped and shook empty beer bottles out the car window trying to urge students to get into the car with them.

Brownese kept her attention focused on school and her lessons. She was much too young to follow Gaye; but out of innocence, Gaye shared many of her mischievous stories with Brownese, especially those dealing with discussions about sex, drinking beer, and illicit talk about boys.

One evening when Gaye returned home from school, Mrs. Bobbitt had sent Sadie, her daughter, to fetch white potatoes and cornmeal from Mama. Gaye and Sadie played for a few minutes until Mama had packaged the items Mrs. Bobbitt asked for. Since Mama didn't have much cornmeal left for herself, she kindly placed a note in the bag asking Mrs. Bobbitt to please return the food she was borrowing.

When Sadie was ready to go home, Gaye persuaded Mama to let her walk halfway home with Sadie. They walked along up the path holding hands until they were out of sight of the house. Before Gaye could tag Sadie and tell her good-bye, Sadie grabbed her arm and pulled her back to whisper something in Gaye's ear. She made Gaye promise that she wouldn't tell anyone what she said. "Show me what you are talking about," Gaye insisted. Sadie pulled Gaye toward her and started kissing her mouth and feeling her breasts.

She and Gaye got down on the ground atop some prickly leaves. Sadie pulled up Gaye's dress, then hers, and lay on top of Gaye. They did a sex act, with Sadie humping up and down, up and down on Gaye. Gaye did not know what to think of this. She hadn't got this feeling with anyone before, but she knew this humping felt good to her. Sadie stroked her vagina tenderly; after the humping stopped, Gaye began to tremble, lying there underneath Sadie.

When Gaye finally pushed Sadie off of her, Gaye ran straight home to tell Brownese that Sadie had lain down on top of her and put her hand in her panties and felt her pee-pee. "It felt soooo good!" Gaye innocently told Brownese, and promised she would show her how to do that so she could feel good, too.

"I'm telling Mama," Brownese cried. Gaye was frightened and definitely would not tell her anything more because she couldn't keep things secret between them. Not wanting to be a tattle-tale, Brownese followed Gaye around the back of the house where no one could see them.

"This is the way she did me," Gaye explained. She tried to repeat for Brownese exactly what Sadie had done to her. She humped up and down on Brownese and tried her best to make Brownese feel good. "Didn't you like that?" Gaye asked Brownese.

"No!" Brownese said. She began to cry, and took off running around the house screaming, "Mama, Mama, Gaye was on top of me." She told Mama that Gaye got down on the ground and moved up and down on top on her. Then she put her hand under my dress, Mama. Mama, trying to get supper ready, paid the girls no attention. She brushed them aside and told Gaye to clean up her room and Brownese to study her schoolwork.

Nita was all grown up now and about ready to start courting. She never liked any of the boys around home, so she told Mama she wanted to drop out of the eleventh grade and leave home. Mama didn't want Nita to drop out of school and leave, but she could not convince her to continue. Ginger and Greta would help out in the field with the chopping as they had done nearly all their lives, having dropped out of school a long time ago. They hadn't even received an elementary school diploma.

Nita went to the city, hopefully to find a job and stay with Mirah until she could find a place of her own. When Nita arrived at Mirah's house, Mirah was packing up her things and getting ready to leave the city within a week for good. She was disgruntled with Nate, her husband, but Nita didn't care because she had met Dan, Nate's brother. They knew it was love at first sight and wasted no time before they were married. Their budding love lasted only a few weeks before they fell into the routine of drinking and attending all the night spots and parties Dan's friends were giving.

One weekend the month following, Nita brought her husband home to meet Mama and Papa. Nita told them that she loved living in the city working as a housemaid. She was getting paid every week and would not be coming home to stay. However low the wages were in the city, Nita didn't even have it in her mind to return to the farm and start chopping cotton and peanuts again.

Nita and Dan began their family of little ones, and they came fast. They had seven babies, and between each one, Dan and she fought each other furiously like cats and dogs and threw hurtful and vulgar cursing words toward each other. The two of them worked hard during the week, but every weekend they loved to get a babysitter for the children and go to a juke joint to drink their money away. No sooner had they arrived home from their drunken binges than they began fighting each other, which lasted until almost daybreak.

The children never had a weekend when their mom and dad weren't fighting. When they grew up, the drunken brawls increased. The fighting attacks usually ended with Nita being rushed to the trauma ward at the nearest hospital many times with her face cut severely and eyes half closed from butcher knife stab wounds Dan had given her. These bruised and bloody episodes sent Nita and Dan's children screaming into the street past midnight begging for someone to please stop their mom and dad from fighting.

Nothing could stop Dan from his vicious ways. He got drunk and stood over Nita one night, cursing her while she nursed their baby. As he viscously beat her over the head with his fist, he pointed a butcher knife at her throat with the other hand, in case she tried to fight back. On one occasion when she threw out her arm to protect her and her baby's face, her hand caught the sharp butcher knife blade, and it sliced off the tip of her thumb that she had burned in the hot ashes when she was just a toddler. Again, Nita was taken to the hospital trauma center, but she never filed charges against her bastard husband Dan for his vicious domestic violence, which lasted nearly all of their married life together.

Mama had tantrums from the trauma Nita was undergoing. She could not figure out why Nita allowed Dan to beat on her. She could come back home to stay, but there was not enough room for her seven children. She just stayed where she was with Dan, trying to please him and make a home for their children. She was trapped. Mama could not think of a way out of this violent situation for Nita until Nita wanted to help herself.

It seemed Mama and Papa's lot was to care for the generations of children in their family. Early in the spring, Mama got a letter from her deaf and dumb cousin Harry asking if he could come to visit her and that he had something he wanted to talk about. Mama had not seen her cousin Harry for years. She knew she had a deaf and dumb cousin, but no one ever spoke to her about him.

During his visit, he told Mama that he was getting divorced and wanted her to care for his two young children, one-year-old Rod and three-year-old Cissy. Mama talked to Harry by writing and reading on paper about their desperate situation on the farm, but she would try to keep the children. She was incapable of turning Harry down because she had handicapped children herself, and she thought it must be hard for him to find work if he can't speak or hear.

Mama and Papa had no idea how they would care for these two children, Rod and Cissy. Harry, their dad, left the two little children penniless with Mama, wearing only the clothes they had on their backs. Life was difficult living on the farm, and Mama and Papa were barely making a living for themselves. They feared getting two more hungry mouths to feed, but Mama took the children in anyway. After clearly expressing their poor existence on the farm to Harry again, he insisted that he would be sending Mama and Papa money to help raise the children.

At first, a few dollars trickled in from Harry; but as the years went by and the children grew up, Mama realized that they had been bated to keep the children when Harry promised her that he would visit them once a month and bring the children money and clothes. There was nothing Harry sent his children to live on, and after about three months passed, he never visited them again. Mama and Papa barely existed themselves; they feared they would continue to grow penniless.

At age six, Cissy started elementary school. She loved school but found it very hard to adjust to her teachers. She had no school books and no one to help her with her lessons. Seeing herself a failure in school, Cissy grew glum and disgruntled as her school years progressed.

Whenever she was asked to help with the housework, clean her room, or wash the dishes, Cissy became angry, rolled her eyes, and screamed, No! She gave Mama an excuse that she had something else to do. When Mama asked her to help out with the farm work or straighten up her room, she always gave Mama sassy talk that led to an ugly spanking. Cissy would have none of it, telling Mama that she wasn't her mama, but she would straighten up her room for a while. No sooner had she forgotten her promise to Mama than she was right back with her disobedience. Cissy stayed in her room and refused to join the family members at dinnertime or at work in the field for most of her teenage years.

Mirah moved back home the following summer; this time for good. She promised Mama she would help with Harry's children, Cissy and Rod, and her her own two children, Maela and Tony. Mirah developed a mean streak after she had lived in the city for a while, and especially after having left her abusive husband Nate and seeing her brother Russ slain.

Mirah began to take over Mama's job of cooking a meal here and there, taking care of the small children, and bossing them around at her convenience. She gave them orders and demands about what chores they were to do around the house. Brownese, Gaye, and Cissy were to work in the house and in the field. Brownese and Gaye could practically look after themselves, since Gaye was well into high school and Brownese, following close behind her, had entered high school as well. Ginger and Greta knew they had to work and didn't need anyone telling them what to do. Mirah went out of her way trying to order Cissy and Rod around. She hounded them if they told her they were not doing any work unless Mama asked them to.

Rod was a frail little boy that everyone loved. He had a sweet smile and was always pleasant to Mama and Papa. He had nothing to do with Cissy and felt that she had been very mean and hateful to Mama and Papa. Rod worked hard on the farm after he became old enough, around thirteen or fourteen years old. As he grew to be a young man, Papa taught him how to plow and hitch up the wagon. He stayed outdoors most of the time, tending to the cattle, mules, and hogs. General farm work was all he knew, so he never developed much liking for schoolwork. As soon as he finished elementary school, he began to work harder and harder on the farm, hoping to get money when the harvest was over. Mama told Rod instances about his sister never helping out with the housework, and honestly, Rod was afraid to say no to Mama and Papa when they asked him to do a job around the house or on the farm. He was so unlike Cissy, and they grew further and further apart after Mama told Rod about her behavior.

Mirah grew jealous of Rod and Cissy, and she started to complain that Mama was giving them more attention than she was her own grandchildren, Maela and Tony. Mirah even took it upon herself to scold Rod and Cissy for trying to go to school and not helping with the farm work. She especially stayed on Cissy's back, ordering her to get to the field to chop cotton and peanuts. Cissy, being a very stubborn and quiet young girl, couldn't get Mirah to stop dogging her and often complained to Mama about how she was being slapped and pushed around. Mama never really paid her complaints much attention because she took them as sibling scraps that happened with Mirah quite frequently, even with Gaye and Brownese. But Cissy didn't see it that way.

Mirah kept up this abuse with Cissy for years, driving her to stay away from home on weekends without telling Mama where she was. These episodes hurt Mama deeply, and she took Cissy's leaving without permission to heart, but she knew Mirah was partly to blame for Cissy's bad behavior. Mirah simply would not stay off Cissy's back. She acted as if she hated her ugly ways for all she was worth.

Amid so much turmoil coming from Mirah, Cissy eventually reached tenth grade, her junior year in high school, and couldn't take Mirah's abuse any longer. She ran away from school and home with a man much older than she was and married him. Mama and Papa neither knew where she was nor what she had done. Cissy just vanished from the family and her brother Rod in a huff with Mirah and never returned.

Mama didn't want Cissy to drop out of high school, but she didn't listen and quit anyway. The quitting didn't stop Mirah's scolding. She continued to argue and fight with Mama shamefully for letting

Cissy leave. She began to run with Papa, spending all his money, which Mama needed for food and clothing for the children. Mirah was definitely a hindrance in the home and caused arguments which led the family to break up. On many occasions, she tried to cover up her wrongdoings, but she would not attend church with Mama or ask forgiveness for her wicked behavior.

After Rod entered high school, it was becoming somewhat difficult for him to continue in school, so he finally dropped out and went to work full-time on the farm. Later, a girlfriend talked him into getting his GED. He had stayed on the farm and worked for many years without the wages he needed to care for himself. When Lola's husband Leland offered him a training job with him in his dry cleaners, he was too glad to pack his things and leave. He stayed with Leland for a few years. During this time, he worked and saved enough money to purchase a cleaning business of his own. Rod became very successful and never forgot his love for Mama and Papa and how they had given him a chance in life, though it was next to nothing.

Mirah stayed on the farm for many years, pretending to help Mama and Papa raise the crops. She took to hanging onto Papa more frequently now, eking every dime from him she could get. Mirah coaxed Papa into buying an old jalopy truck with what little money he had, and she drove him to and from town on weekends. These were the times when Mirah forced Papa to spend his money he borrowed for crop seeds on whisky and beer. Having done this, she and Papa would return home from town drunk and empty-handed. Mama often argued with both of them and scolded Mirah about being away all day long and half of the night. Each time she did this, Mama cared for her children alone while Mirah was gallivanting in the street, drinking whisky with Papa. Mama often told Papa he should be ashamed of himself, running with his daughter Mirah, who had two children of her own and wasn't doing anything to help raise them.

If Mirah was drunk When Mama said these things to her, Mirah started cursing Mama and dogging her around as well. Mama went into her shell, while Mirah, with her drunken self, threatened to beat Mama with a piece of stove wood she picked up off the floor and aimed at her. Many times Mirah offered to fight with Mama if she didn't leave her alone and shut her mouth. There was no stopping Mirah; she was definitely out of control, and the whisky drinking left the entire household in shambles, penniless, and her children, Maela and Tony frightened.

Maela was growing tall and enjoying her first year of high school life. She studied hard and told Mama and Papa she wanted to go to college. Maela never missed a day of school and loved living with Grandma and Grandpa on the farm. There, under the guidance of her mother Mirah she could do no harm, often fearful of how Mirah was treating her grandma. Mirah tried to help out, but whatever good work she did was destroyed on the weekend when she let her children go unattended.

Mirah never cared much for her son, Tony, so he more or less took care of himself. He was an innocent and expressionless child who was fearful of his mother. He often found a quiet spot in his grandma's lap, especially while Mirah cussed and fought with the other children and chased them up and down the stairs to wait on her and do menial chores around the house. Her two children had no excitement in their lives, except for school, and Mirah had nothing to do with making life happy and comfortable for them while they were living there with Mama and Papa.

Around Christmastime, it was Mama who tried to give Mirah's children gifts and bits of good food to eat. Her daughters in the city sent her presents for Christmas, so she used whatever money she had to make sure Santa Claus came to visit the grandchildren each year.

Papa's peanut allotment had been cut almost in half, and he thought about raising some other type crop that would bring him an income equal to the peanut profits he would not be receiving. He spoke with other farmers in the area who had experienced cutbacks on peanut crops as well.

One of his neighbors over on another farm confided in Papa that he would teach him how to raise tobacco in exchange for some free hands to help him harvest his crop that year. Now, Papa knew he wanted a different crop, but tobacco was far from his mind, especially if he had to swap his family workers for labor to help raise tobacco.

Papa thought about the hands he had to help with the crops. He could count on Mama, Greta, Ginger, himself, and sometimes Mirah, Ed, and Van. Gaye was a junior in college, and Brownese was heavily into finishing her high school work and applying for college in the fall. Besides, Mama would not let them skip days from school to work on the farm. Maela and Tony were much too young to work in the field. It would be a hindrance for anyone to teach them how. Mama told Papa this before he made up his mind to raise the tobacco crop.

For a while, Papa tried to coax Nita to return to the farm to help out, but she never came. He would be forced to harvest his tobacco crop without the women who had already left home. But he wondered about the tobacco process itself.

Van ran with a woman on weekends and gave her most of his money that was left from his buying whisky and keeping his old jalopy car running. He never worked much in the fields after he bought a car because his drinking problem extended into weekdays, and very little farm work was ever done. The money he received from attending veteran's school was spent the same week he received it; and when it was, he came home and waited until the next check arrived. Whenever Papa spoke to him about the work on the farm, Van argued with him, saying that he wanted to leave and was tired of farm work. Papa certainly could not count on him to help with raising tobacco, but he did stay for the harvesting season.

The process of raising tobacco was not an easy task. Papa had to purchase hybrid seeds so they would bring forth healthy plants. After the tobacco seeds were planted, he needed to cover the seed beds with rolls of stretched cheese cloth so they would be protected from the harsh, flooding spring rains and heavy winds that could sweep away the seeds. Papa peeked underneath the cover two or three times a week to make sure the seeds were breaking through the ground and progressing into larger, healthier plants. As soon as these plants had about eight inches of growth, they were ready to be set out in the long bedded rows and cultivated so they could grow into mature plants. Then they were left to ripen from the bottom up on the stalks in the field.

Without notice, sometimes hailstorms attacked the young plants and left holes in the leaves. At other times, and before the leaves had fully ripened, tobacco worms feasted on the tender plants. They chewed the leaves until they were stripped if they were not dusted to keep away the pests. Papa was not prepared to keep the worms from attacking the tobacco plants. Having no money to get the plants dusted, all the workers had to help de-worm the tobacco plants one by one to rid them of the green, plump, horny worms that filled their bellies to capacity feeding off the juicy plants. With a two-pronged stick, the worms were plucked from the tobacco leaves, smashed on the ground, and killed. Sometimes, they were collected in a bucket and dumped in a hole in the ground that had been filled with poison dust. This process sickened the workers, but if it hadn't been thoroughly handled, the horned worms would have nibbled the leaves completely.

Papa needed to build a barn with a good flue, where he would hang the ripe leaves to cure at a temperature cranked up to about 350 degrees for two or three weeks. This expense was not expected, so Papa bought on credit the lumber and tobacco racks he needed to cure the tobacco.

After the tobacco started ripening in the field, work got underway gathering the leaves from the stalks. Waiting any longer would be risky, so Papa warned everyone that the tobacco crop was ready to be harvested and cured. Papa and Van struggled for three or four weeks gathering the ripe tobacco leaves from the field. Papa built a sleigh with canvas on each side that Lucy pulled between the narrow rows. The ripe tobacco leaves were gathered week by week on the sleigh until the harvesting was completed.

After the tobacco leaves were taken from the field, Mama and Ginger handed a bunch containing three or four leaves to Greta or Mirah, who looped them tightly around some poles and hung them outside on racks until all the ripe leaves had been gathered. After this process had ended, the tobacco leaves were put into the barn and flue cured for the market.

The temperature in the barn had to be set right for an even cure. Papa stayed up each night during the curing process to check the temperature and stoke the fire every three hours to make sure the heat for the curing process was kept temperate. Mama worked hard helping Papa to cure the tobacco. She stayed awake, too; for she worried that Papa would fall asleep and ruin the whole cur-ing process, which would decrease the amount the market would pay for his crop. When the leaves that were being cured turned a medium brown in the barn, Papa, Ed, and Van took them out and placed them under a shed until they got enough tobacco racks stacked for a wagon load. Then Papa and Van took the wagon load of cured leaves to the tobacco market. They stayed at the market, some-times overnight, until the tobacco received bids, depending mostly on the grade and how evenly it was cured.

Papa's tobacco was most nearly auctioned last, no matter how early he arrived at the market. He also could depend on the white farmers' tobacco crops almost always receiving a better rating than his. He was afraid to complain, and he often told the merchants that he was sharecropping for a Mr. Dandridge and was sent to the market with a load of tobacco. This lie nearly always garnered Papa a slightly above-average price at the market. He remained submissive as he waited, listening to the merchants bidding on his tobacco. Oftentimes, low prices angered Papa deeply, and he always left the market with a lower price than what he had hoped for.

After the tobacco crop had been gathered, cured, and taken to the market, Van and Papa had money and time on their hands to visit the other part of the family that had moved away to the city. Once they arrived, they went to all the night spots and spent all the money made from the tobacco crop, save the few dollars Mama asked Papa for food and clothes for Mirah's children. She also asked for tuition fees for Gaye, who would be graduating from college in the spring, and for Brownese, who would be entering her sophomore college year.

After a few days in the city, Papa and Van were ready to return home; but not without buying a bottle of whisky, which he and Papa drank while they were driving back home. Papa had developed some type of urinary leaking problem, Van thought, because no sooner had they gotten a good start on the road home than Papa had to stop every twenty miles or more by the roadside and make a mad dash for the bushes and relieve himself of the alcohol he had been drinking.

After Van, like Papa, had become sufficiently drunk, Van's driving became more and more erratic. In an instant, it seemed, he hit a car head-on and killed the driver while he was trying to overtake a vehicle on the right. Not knowing what to do, and frightened about what he had done, Van went into spasms. He and Papa both escaped to the woods where they hid until daybreak. After daylight came, and seeing that the police had taken away the dead man and the car he was driving, Van and Papa sneaked back to the car, started it up, and drove home with the left fender hanging off and the head-light broken. After Papa and Van had sobered from drinking, they were too ashamed to report to the sheriff what they had done.

When they pulled into the yard three days later, Mama could see that they had wrecked the car. After Papa told her what happened, she knew the sheriff would track them down, so she was frightened that Van would have to pay for killing someone with his car. Van hid the car on the farm property in the back field behind some trees and bushes and left it there to rust away, for fear someone would know who committed the terrible crime.

Early the next day, Papa and Van and caught the Greyhound bus to town. They needed to act fast because Mama told Van that if he didn't have insurance on his car, he was going to pay for the accident that killed a man. They rushed to the clerk's office in town and asked the secretary to take Van's name off the deed to the farm property and put Papa's name on the new one. The court did not know Van had taken the life of a man while drunk driving.

Sure enough, the sheriff traced Van to his house, but Van was able to escape to the woods and hide so no one could see where he was, not even Mama and Papa. As soon as the sheriff left the house, Van returned from the woods. He gathered his belongings and took off to the city for good to live with Hugh. It was the last time Van worked on the farm, and the last time the sheriff came to the house looking for him. Van's crime went unpunished, and Papa's property was never taken to pay the debt.

Mama was not pleased at all to see Van go to live with Hugh because Hugh had just returned from the penitentiary for selling moonshine whisky. Hugh's life was in shambles, and when he went to prison, his wife Mabel left him and took their three children with her. Mabel stayed with Mama for several months until she and the children moved to another town across the state line, where Mabel's family lived.

Work on the tobacco farm continued, yet Papa wondered how he could keep the farm afloat after Van left home. Ed took a part-time sawmill job when he was idle during the fall and winter months. Each day he complained about Van leaving home. Most of the farm women were slowly disappearing from farm life, except for Gaye and Brownese, who were in college. The women looked for marriage and quick fortunes in the city. At times, it forced the farming to come to a complete standstill, leaving all the harvesting tobacco for Mama, Mirah, Greta, and Ginger to do.

Papa knew that farm life had just about ended for him. His one mule Ginny had aged and was no longer strong enough to plow the long rows in the fields. Papa gave her away to a neighbor farmer who lived down the road. He used the mule for light gardening and for pulling a wagon. He kept Lucy because she would be used to plow the tobacco field and the garden. The one cow and several hogs left in the barnyard were slaughtered. The meat was cured in the smokehouse and stored for later use.

Mirah especially was often disgruntled and gave Papa little help with the tobacco harvesting. She used the excuse that she had to do house work and care for the children too. Mama told her that she always managed to have something else to do or somewhere to go when it came time for harvesting the tobacco, leaving Maela and Tony at home for her to care for. Mama demanded that Papa would not be using Gaye and Brownese to help raise tobacco crops and that she intended to let them not only continue college but also to graduate.

VII. DESTINY RULES

When Gaye graduated from college and left home, Brownese had two more years of studying before finishing college. She and Gaye had become close throughout high school and college, and now, Brownese was left alone to finish college. Knowing that she would see Gaye only during her college breaks, Brownese worked hard to complete her own college career.

Gaye studied hard for her classes in college and loved the social activities with the fraternity boys and sorority girls. As soon as it was time for her to graduate, she dreaded leaving college life behind and returning home to work in the field. She tried, at least, to give Mama and Papa another field hand. Seeing how Gaye helped out with the work load, Mama and Papa hoped she would decide to take a job teaching at home so she could help them do the farm work.

Gaye wrapped herself around Mirah's two children, Maela and Tony, and tried to be a mother to them. She bought them toys at Christmas, cute clothes, and saw to it that they stayed in school. Gaye was determined that these young children would not work in the field as she had done. Each summer during school breaks, Gaye continued to take care of Mirah's children as well as she encouraged Brownese to remain in college until she graduates. She wanted to devote most of her time to the young children.

Gaye's first job after graduating from the segregated state college was teaching at an elementary school near home, where she attended high school. She used her first check to buy Mama a washing machine and her sisters Greta and Ginger hearing aids. Gaye was always trying to make life for them more pleasant for her family because she knew Mama and Papa did not have the money to spend on Greta and Ginger. With the money Gaye saved, she bought herself a new power glide Chevrolet so she could drive back and forth to her job. She never had problems with her car, so she kept it on the road. She drove her friends around, and drank beer and whisky in her car with various men and women.

Once she stayed out so late that Mama asked Mirah to use Papa's old jalopy truck to take her to look for Gaye. No sooner had they gotten to the store down the road than they saw Gaye's car. "She has parked it by a roadside store and left in someone else's car," Mama Thought, as she and Mirah sat there waiting for whoever took Gaye out to drive up.

Mama and Mirah waited there until the early morning hours before the car drove up that took Gaye out. They ducked down in the seat whenever they heard a car coming; after the car passed, they sat up when it faded out of sight. Sitting there quietly for hours, finally, when a car drove up and stopped, they rose up from their seat to stare underneath the highway lights when they heard a car door slam. "I wonder who picked up Gaye," Mama said. She was speechless when Gaye jumped out of Mr. Gadsen's car, a white man who operated the service station. If anyone found out she had been with Mr. Gadsen, she would be murdered or her teaching job taken away from her.

Mirah and Mama followed Gaye home, and arrived there only a few minutes later than Gaye did. Mama called Gaye into her room to scold her harshly about what she had seen and who she was with.

Gaye was too frightened to tell Mama that Mr. Gadsen bought beer for them to drink in his car. As she sat there with him in the dark, he suddenly started the car running. Before she could get out of his car, he was heading down the road. She asked him where he was going, but he didn't answer and just drove on. They stopped in a wooded area where no one could see them and forced her to have sex with him. Standing there in front of Mama, she thought how helpless she had been to get away from him. Gaye cried after Mama gave her a harsh scolding and complained to her that there was no social life at home for her. She promised Mama she would never be caught out at night with a white man again.

Five months later, Gaye noticed that her stomach was growing big. She thought she was pregnant because she hadn't gotten a menstrual period after she had sex with Mr. Gadsen on the back seat of his car. She painfully realized that Mr. Gadsen, a white man, had raped her; now, she was frightened and pregnant. Knowing she wasn't allowed to birth a white man's baby, she left school on a Friday afternoon and headed for the city where Nita lived in search of someone who could abort her baby.

The following Saturday night, Nita took Gaye to a shabby storefront juke joint, where she and Nita entered through the back door. She sat there in a dimly lit pit quietly, until a tall Negro lady, wearing a red bandana wrapped around her head, flung the door open and walked in. She stared at Gaye's stomach and asked her if she was the woman who wanted to get rid of her baby. Nearly in tears and frightened, Gaye answered yes in a squeaky, trembling voice.

The woman threw a dingy white sheet across the table and told Gaye to lie down on top the table. Then she grabbed Gaye's ankles and spread her legs as wide as she could. Gaye's fearful eyes bulged as they followed the woman across the room. She pulled out a long, slender, syringe hidden underneath some rags in the dresser drawer. Using the syringe carefully, the woman sucked some kind of murky fluid from a vinegar bottle on top the dresser. She walked toward the table and stretched again wide open Gaye's legs and said, "This won't hurt." She pushed the syringe deep into Gaye's womb, and within minutes the murky fluid was released. Meanwhile, Gaye lay silently on the table, frozen in fear.

Yanking the syringe from her vagina, the woman said, "That will be fifteen dollars." Gaye paid the woman and got down from the table. She pulled a bunch of rags from her pocketbook and crammed them in her panties between her legs and walked out into the black night with Nita beside her, holding her hand and trying to comfort her.

The next day the blood began to flow from Gaye's womb. She wished she could stop bleeding, but not before the tiny little form trying to survive inside her womb had expelled itself. Gaye returned home Sunday night, without Mama and Papa knowing where she had been. After she crept back into the house, Mirah asked her where she had been all weekend. She told her that Mr. Gadson had raped her and made her pregnant the night she and Mama came looking for her at the store. "I stayed with Nita over the weekend," she told Mirah. "Nita took me to someone who could abort his baby. After that, I came straight home."

Ginger left home the same year Gaye got her first job teaching to live with Nita in the city and to look for a job. Being uneducated, Nita tried to discourage Ginger from coming, for fear she would become a victim in the city. But Ginger went anyway and settled for a job as a domestic worker.

She didn't qualify for any type of professional work, and could only do menial tasks. Her condition, such as it was, would not allow her to return to school. She could not hear or understand what people were talking about.

Ginger was introduced to a man, Wynn, whom she thought would be kind to her. He knew that she was uneducated and knew nothing about courting, marrying, and raising a family. All her life she had worked on the farm since childhood, and she had no knowledge of city slickers and their loutish ways.

As soon as Wynn asked her to marry him, she said yes. Ginger didn't stay with Wynn long because she became frustrated with his violent temper. Seeing how Nita and Dan fought each other the way they did, she did not want that to happen to her. Ginger and Wynn argued and fought for a few years, and finally they got divorced.

Ginger met another man while she was living in the city that she thought could be her perfect partner. She wanted nothing more than for her marriage to work, but Jim was just plain crazy, she often said. He took her to Florida, where she knew no one, to pick oranges in the orchards and gather field peas like a migrant worker. She didn't like it there, and promised herself that if she could ever get back home, she would never return to Florida again.

On occasions, Jim locked her out of the apartment for no reason at all, took her car keys away from her, and hid them so she couldn't go to her day job. These hateful things he did to her were mean and evil although he was declared insane by everyone who knew him. Jim didn't believe in family life and never wanted to attend church with Ginger. He told her he wasn't going to take her anywhere and wasn't going to be seen with her because of her speech and slight of hearing.

One Saturday night, Jim went out and got drunk, came home, and tried to start a fight with Ginger.

Often when he talked to her, she didn't even understand what he was saying. Then he became angry when she wouldn't answer his foolish questions or give-in to his plea for drunken sex.

When Jim came home from work the next Saturday night, he was drunk again. He staggered to the table for his supper; after they ate, they both sat up for a while talking and arguing back and forth about his drinking and their lives together. Later on that night, around ten o'clock, Ginger and Jim went to bed. After she fell asleep, Jim sneaked out of bed, took his pistol from its hiding place in the closet, and placed it under his pillow. He wrestled in bed and bounced up and down on the mattress to see if he could arouse Ginger. Seeing her lying there still and quietly breathing with a light snore, he slid the pistol from underneath his pillow, and placed it between the sheets near Ginger's head, being careful not to awaken her. Without moving or saying a word, Jim fired a shot aimed at Ginger's head that roared throughout the house. Then, aiming the gun at his head, Jim shot and killed himself instantly.

When Ginger's severe pain aroused her from sleep the next morning, she was terrified at what Jim had done to her. He was stretched out lifeless beside her in a pool of blood draining from his mouth and ears. After running out into the street begging for help, someone called an ambulance that took Ginger to the hospital trauma center. After the doctor examined her head, he found that a bullet had lodged itself in her skull behind her right ear. He convinced Ginger to leave the bullet where it was positioned because trying to remove it could cause her to become paralyzed. The bleeding in her head had stopped, so the doctor bandaged the gunshot wound and sent Ginger home. When Ginger returned home from the doctor, she called to have his body picked up.

There was no compensation for this tragic incident. There was no insurance coverage, either, and no justification for this terrible act Jim had committed. Ginger's life went downhill for years to come because she never recovered fully from the gun shot blow to her head. She was able to do light housekeeping and cleaning, but could not forget that horrible night which left her speech more jumbled than ever before.

In later years, Ginger developed paralysis in her hands and shoulders and was no longer able to hold a steady job. Acute dementia took its toll on her also, and she became less and less able to recognize her immediate surroundings. At times Ginger went the opposite way home and a policeman would have to escort her back to her home address, which he was able to see on her driver's license. She became unable to operate a car as well. It was hard for Ginger to give up her car, but she had no choice.

Mama did not take this shooting too lightly. She, Greta, and Gaye went to see Ginger and tried to get her to return home, but she couldn't because of her day job. After Mama had given her a good lecture, they returned home and reported to Papa that Ginger had nearly lost her life.

Brownese was entering her junior year in college when Papa had no options but to repair and renovate the old house they were living in. The weatherboard had rotted, and the leaking tin roof was getting worse. It caused the inside of the kitchen and upstairs bedrooms to start rotting. The old chimney had nearly fallen over. Times were tough, but Papa managed to get one good harvest from the tobacco crops before he decided to hire a contractor to rebuild a better two-story house. When the money ran out, the house was left partly unfinished upstairs. Papa bought ply board and covered the bare walls himself.

When Brownese went back to college that fall, the income from tobacco was barely enough to pay the remainder of her tuition, but when she was offered a part-time job on campus, she stayed in college. During the summers, she waited tables up north for wages and tips in a summer spa, trying to make enough money to buy books and school clothes.

Gaye loved teaching the children in her class, and they loved her although she didn't have children of her own. Her teaching career led to permissiveness with married men, and she listened to them tell her stories about the drunken brawls with their wives. These men never respected Gaye as a lady but as a sex partner and a drinking pal. This behavior continued throughout her teaching job near home.

Whenever Gaye told Brownese these horrible stories about herself, Brownese began to stay away from Gaye. She felt guilty about the way she regarded Gaye, and she tried to tell her that her life was moving in the wrong direction. Gaye was a good woman, especially to Brownese when she was in college. Knowing she didn't have anything extra to help keep her in college, she received packages from Gaye with cookies, peanuts, and apples in them. Often she got letters from Gaye with one or two dollars to buy snacks.

When Gaye grew tired of men chasing after her and wanted to settle down, she found a man,

Jonas, who was hired to help renovate Papa's family home. On weekends, when he was not working, they started dating regularly. They courted for a very short time before Jonas got drafted into the army. When he was about ready to leave, he told Gaye he was going into the army and asked her if she would marry him before he left.

Gaye was hesitant to say yes, because she wanted a wedding, but she didn't want it to be in a church; there was no time before Jonas would be leaving. They found a minister who would perform a simple wedding ceremony and got married at his sister's house.

Gaye and Jonas lived with his sister and her husband until it was time for Jonas to go to the army. Gaye stayed with them for a short while after Jonas left because his sister and her husband were evil and mean to Gaye. She often came home on weekends to tell Mama how nasty they were treating her. They made her buy groceries for herself and then used them for their own family. She was not allowed to use the kitchen until certain hours and had limited access to the bathroom. Gaye, not being able to withstand the harsh treatment, moved out of his sister's house into an apartment of her own and never went back. Jonas never forgave Gaye for leaving his sister's home while he was away, as if he needed her to spy on his wife.

One weekend Gaye took Greta to visit Ginger in the city. She had her heart set on meeting some-one special and getting a good job. Although she went back to school to learn to read and write, she was not able to get professional jobs because of her speech and hearing impediment. She was a hard worker and felt happy that she would be near her sister Ginger. They supported and protected each other, and they traveled back and forth home often to make sure Mama and Papa were doing well and to take them a few dollars.

Greta met Ginger's ex-husband's brother, Hayden. They became attached to one another; he was a preacher, and she was an avid church lady and immaculate housekeeper. Greta knew this was the man for her, so she decided to stay in the city longer just to be with Hayden.

After Hayden and Greta married, Greta suffered a false pregnancy, which turned out to be a tumor in her stomach. After surgery, she became pregnant again, this time with a beautiful boy. Her next child was a cute little girl; Gena, she called her.

Greta was overjoyed to have her own home and family, and she was even happier when they moved into their new house they had built on her husband's inherited property. Her pride was sending her children to school, working in the cafeteria to help put them through college, and volunteering at her church. College life took the children away, but Greta never did lose touch with them. While they were away, she kept herself busy growing a rich vegetable garden, which she shared with all the neighbors. She washed, ironed, and cleaned for her husband; nothing was too good for Greta's family. She was much like Mama and tried to give her children just as much love as Mama had given her. When her children graduated from college, they stayed in the town with Greta so they could be near their mama and help take care of her.

Mama's load never left her shoulders; from morning until dusk she worked in the tobacco field, trying her best to make a living and replace the work hands the women had taken away from her. She was growing old and tired now, after raising three sets of children and working in the field all day. All the women had drifted off to the city, except for Mirah and her two children, Maela and Tony. Mirah's children were not suited to work in the field, so they went to school instead of helping Mama out at home. Gaye took a job teaching in another town up north and Brownese was about ready to finish college.

Ed complained often about all the women leaving home and that he had the work do. He was always disgruntled, and Papa could look in his face and tell that he was angry most of the time. Papa continued to work his last crop in the tobacco fields, hoping to raise enough money to see Brownese finish her senior year of college and get a job teaching as well. She convinced Mama that she loved college and wanted to continue on and make something of herself.

During the planting season, it was not so hard for Papa and Ed to do the work. During the summers when the tobacco needed plowing, Ed helped Papa to do most of it. Mirah and Mama wished for help taking in the tobacco from the field, but they had no way to return the labor and no money to hire help for a day's work. Often the neighbors took pity on Mama and helped her finish the tobacco crop without pay.

Mama tried to get rest during the winter and spring months. During this time she visited Lola in the city on many occasions. The children, in turn, came home to visit Mama at Christmas, Easter, and Mother's Day. Each time they came, they brought her lovely gifts, but money was what she needed most.

Having grown tired and aged, Mama's heart grew faint. She ached with fierce pain that brought on a heart attack, straining her fainting breath from her body. As the days went by, and she was not feeling better, Mirah phoned Gaye, Brownese, and Lola to tell them that Mama was seriously ill and had been taken to the hospital. No one called Nita, Ginger, and Greta to let them know Mama had been in the hospital, and they never forgave Mirah for not letting them know Mama was ill.

All her children rushed home, except Hugh, who was serving his second term in the state institution for selling moonshine whisky. No sooner had everyone arrived than Mama was well enough to come home—so we all thought. When she was discharged from the hospital, the doctors gave her specific orders to stay in bed.

Lola and Gaye decided to stay at home for a week to take care of Mama and nurse her back to health, but some of the other women left because they needed to be at work on Monday Morning. Lola cooked nourishing soups and served them to Mama in bed, hoping Mama would get well. She had been with Mama a few hours after Brownese was born, and now she was at home trying her best to comfort Mama during her illness. Lola sat on the side of the bed and gazed into Mama's eyes and listened for any little sign of improvement in her breathing.

Taking her eyes off Mama for just one moment, she heard a loud pop that sounded like a light bulb had exploded. Flashing her eyes toward Mama, she glared at her face as her last breath escaped hastily from her chest. In an instant, Mama had passed away. Lola grabbed Mama, put her arms around her shoulders, and shook her vigorously to get her breathing again. Lola could not bear the pain seeing Mama take her last breath. She knew instantly that the loud pop she heard was a signal from God that Mama had gone home to rest with Him.

Gaye bathed Mama gently and put a pretty white gown on her. Then she drove to town to ask the undertaker to pick up Mama's body and carry her away. Everyone in the household and those who had to be called back home broke into wailing and weeping for dear Mama. She was at peace now, her toil of a lifetime behind her. No one wanted to wait for what would happen next.

All the children came to Mama's funeral, even Cissy, who only stayed there briefly without speaking to anyone. Hugh was escorted home with state prison officials and had to leave immediately after the funeral. Mama did not want to be buried at the back gate where Papa's mammy and pappy were. She made it clear to her daughters that she wanted to be buried underneath the mystic cedar tree at the top of the path where she had seen the light shoot up from the ground. She hoped that one day the light would come down to earth and lift her to heaven. Papa instructed the gravediggers to prepare the place where Mama requested to be buried.

Papa never did do much farming after Mama passed, so Mirah stayed on at home for about two or three years, helping him to adjust to Mama being gone. Papa didn't want to do without Mama by his side. His ability to work on the farm had declined.

Growing old and feeble, he barely could take care of himself and was not feeling up to doing any work at all. He took to sitting around the house all day, and mostly staying in bed from sunup to sundown.

Mirah was there to help him and to keep her children in school. She often went away for long weekends, leaving Maela and Tony to cook and care for Papa as best they could. When Nate, Mirah's husband, found out she was abandoning the children on weekends, he stole Tony from Mirah when he was at Papa's house and took him away to live with him in the city up north and never brought him back. Maela, being a senior in high school, would not leave, so she took care of herself and Papa when her mom, Mirah, was away. Whenever Mirah came home, she got into dogging Maela and making her work inside the house, often on her hands and knees scrubbing the floors.

Mirah knew Papa was not able to work, so she helped him to apply for social security benefits. The reason she wanted Papa to get help was because she knew she could talk Papa out of every cent he owned, and she did just that. She waited patiently each month for his check to arrive. When Mirah cashed Papa's check for him, she pretended that what she bought for herself was also for Papa. With each passing day, Papa became frailer although Mirah was supposed to be caring for him. Mirah helped him to sell the usable farm equipment to other farmers in the area, and the one mule Lucy, who was left alone in the stable without any work to do. Papa used the money the sale brought to help settle some of his debts.

One weekend when Gaye came to visit Papa, she insisted that she was taking Papa to the city with her and keeping him there until she could get him the care he needed, even if he had to go into a nursing home. That way, she would be close to Papa and could visit him during the week.

During his short stay at the nursing home, and after many tests to find out which facility he needed to go to, the doctors discovered that Papa had caught tuberculosis and would be sent to a sanitarium. When Gaye heard about this, she and Brownese went to see Papa in the sanitarium to find out exactly what had happened to him and how he was being treated.

When Mirah discovered that Papa was in the sanitarium and would not be coming home again, Mirah left home seeking a weird religious cult, unlike the Baptist church to which she had belonged all her life. This religious cult persuaded Mirah to close Papa's house. They found a job as maid for her near where they lived in New York. She moved all of Papa's furniture, and what she didn't want she gave to the people in her religious cult. She left very little for Ed to survive on, since he was the only one left at home. Papa stayed in the sanitarium a couple of years, but the disease increased and spread throughout his lungs. As he grew older, it finally took his life.

After Papa passed away, Mirah could not be found. Gaye and Lola sought agencies in New York and family members to help find her, but no one had an address showing where she lived. Mirah never forgave her family for not letting her know that Papa had died and was buried. Her heart was broken and empty because she was not able to say good-bye to Papa. To this day, Mirah accuses her family members for making this painful mistake, regardless of whether or not anyone knew where she lived.

Brownese finished college and took a job teaching close to where Gaye lived. She was not able to help Mama and Papa much during their older years, for she had only just begun her career after they both had passed away.

Maela had finished high school and was getting ready for college in the fall. She left home to live with Gaye, who took full responsibility for her entering college. After four years had passed, Maela graduated from college and began teaching.

It was Lola's job to try to keep the family's property out of debt because of unpaid loans that Mirah had failed to pay out of the social security income Papa was receiving. A short time after Papa became ill and was not able to work; Mirah sold her share of the inherited property to a white man, Mr. Centure. When Lola discovered what had happened, she confronted Mirah about the sale and hoped she would take responsibility for the bills she created on the property. Mirah exclaimed, "I don't want anything to do with it." Hearing this, Lola got her sisters and brothers together to help pay off the debts so the lien on the property would be clear and free. Many of the sisters and brothers took this responsibility lightly, and would not pay the debt. Lola became very angry because she constantly had to prod each one of her sisters and brothers for an agreed amount each promised to pay before the bank could clear the debt. She warned her brothers and sisters that if they did not pay their share, they would be left off the deed to the property. Lola kept her word. Those who helped to settle the farm lien received deeds to the ownership of the property. Those who did not help disinherited their share of Papa's property. A deed was written and distributed to each of the family members who had paid their share of the debt. Only four of the seven women and none of the men received deeds to the property the family was about to lose.

When Gaye and Jonas were tired of moving from one apartment to another, they purchased a lot and built a beautiful house in the city. After being in their house for a few months, they held a lovely housewarming to show off their beautifully decorated home.

Gaye had many new friends in her community and at school. Her time was so intensely occupied with teaching that she was unable to care for her home properly. Jonas was mean to Gaye because she was never home and spent all her time with schoolwork, but he also had a job as a cement finisher.

Gaye's pride and joy was Maela and helping her to get her college degree. She wanted Maela to become a success in life and to enjoy the things that she never had as a child, if given the opportunity. When Maela got married, Gaye planned her wedding and saw to it that she had a reception at her home on her beautiful lawn as if Maela was her own daughter.

A huge portion of Gaye's married life led to fighting with Jonas. He would lock her out the house and no sooner had he done this than she broke a basement window in her own home and forced her way back into the house. They had gotten into a fight when he ordered her to leave his home. When she would not leave, he called the authorities and had her admitted to a mental institution for breaking into her own home she had been locked out of. She stayed at that facility for two weeks and was not able to keep her job teaching. Lola and Brownese took turns visiting Gaye and made sure she would be returning home.

To gain more knowledge about teaching, Gaye enrolled in summer school each year at the local university to study for her master's degree in education, which took up most of her time during summer breaks.

After enrolling in school for quite a few semesters, and toward the end of her master's degree,

Gaye wanted to adopt a child, hoping this would improve her and Jonas's relationship and bring them closer to each other. She also wanted more than anything to be successful in her new teaching position and to use all the knowledge she had gained toward her profession.

Her life had drastically taken a turn after she left the mentally ill facility, and she devoted her time to studying, and her new teaching job. When she and Jonas were interviewed for the adoption of a child, the agency offered them two children instead of one. This upset Jonas somewhat, but when he found out the two children were siblings needing adoption, his heart softened. Gaye was overcome with joy, and she was happy just taking care of their two adopted children and teaching.

Mental stress seemed to be working its way into Gaye's life and overcoming her ability to rationalize, which drastically affected her physical ability. One icy winter morning as she was riding to her Saturday class at the university in a carpool with a group of teachers, the driver hit a patch of black ice that spun the car out of control to meet an oncoming vehicle head-on. It was a terrible accident that frightened Gaye to death—she died instantly of cardiac arrest and a broken neck. The night before this accident, a young Negro teenage thug had tried to snatch her pocketbook. Although Gaye hung on to it, her thumb was fractured while she struggled to keep her purse. Seeing her resting there in her casket with a fractured thumb visibly showing, she was a beautiful woman and perfectly peaceful. Her turmoil, at least with Jonas, was gone forever.

Gaye's passing left a big, hurting place in her family and friends' hearts that no one could ever fill. She had been the one to keep the family together and to care for Mama and Papa until they passed away. Gaye even helped her brothers and sisters to keep in touch with each other, but she never could get Mirah into the fold. Much to the family's surprise, Ed told everyone that Jonas killed his sister; no one ever disputed him.

Nita had raised seven children amid turmoil and trauma. Her physical body began to crumble, probably from years of drinking beer and poor nutrition for herself and her family. Dan, her husband, had a responsible job as a plumber, but he did not discipline the children; that was Nita's job. As soon as her children were out of high school, they left home and, without supervision, became victims of rugged city life and the ugliness in their immediate families.

Nita looked healthy, but she developed serious kidney failure and attempted to receive a kidney transplant, which her body rejected. After the operation, she slipped away quietly as she struggled to regain consciousness from a coma. Dan married again, but he never abused his second wife the way he had dogged Nita and their children. Dan inherited Nita's share of the property Papa left to her, which he spent on himself and his new wife. He never offered his children one thin dime. His children never forgave their dad for his behavior. Before long the relationship they had with him drifted away.

Soon after Nita had passed away, Lola lost her husband, Leland. He suffered a devastating heart attack that took his life within a matter of days. Lola, not being able to survive without him, took to drinking heavily, trying to drown the sorrow she felt for the loss of her husband. When she realized that she had been left with a dry-cleaning business, hundreds of acres of land, and cash money, she regained her senses and assessed her wealth.

Lola's one downfall was sordid men and her lack of love for her family. She had cheated on her husband, Leland, as he had cheated on her. One incident led to another that turned out to nearly break up their marriage, especially the day when Lola came home early from her job and discovered her best friend in bed with her husband Leland. This incident gave Lola more fire to step up her unfaithfulness to her husband, and she hung out with other men more frequently.

As the years went by, and as each one of Lola's men and women friends passed away, she took on new ones in their places. There was no discretion about these men being married or single; she had learned to keep a relationship with her friends' husbands without their wives finding out. Mainly, they bought whisky for her, and she sat down at her kitchen table and drank it with them.

After Leland passed away, Lola spent nearly all her wealth on fine clothes, fur coats, cars, and whisky. Nothing would stop her until she met a man whom she let move in with her and who promised to give her anything she wanted. She fell for his fancy talk, and they soon got married. She was sorry afterwards, because she learned that the old rascal had no income at all. He became Lola's dependent, eking a living off her. This worried Lola, and caused her to step up her whisky drinking while trying to release her stress. She became a closet alcoholic and began to stay home and in bed all day, getting up only to take a drink of whisky at will. She sold the cleaning business to help support herself and her new husband, but the money she received from the sale soon gave out.

Mirah especially grew to hate Lola as much as Lola hated her. She often accused Lola of telling her family lies about her cheating Papa out of his money for her personal needs. Lola knew what Mirah was up to because she bought whisky for both Papa and Ed, and now that Papa had passed on, she continued her devilish ways with Ed. She stayed in the old rundown farmhouse with Ed until Lola decided to buy Ed a trailer and had it set on the farm property so he would have access to a decent living.

Lola's sisters and brothers were never welcomed into her beautiful and exclusive home, nor did she offer them any of her wealth and high living. She always felt they were not worthy of what she had. It was no wonder she wrote a will leaving all her assets to her second husband, who had dogged her all during their married life, especially during her illness. She felt he deserved her inheritance more than her own family.

Lola let her health problems get the best of her. She hardly ever went to the doctor or dentist.

She had to get all her teeth pulled, as they began to deteriorate from the whisky drinking. She had never taken a gynecology exam and didn't even know what that was. When she went to see a doctor because she was feeling ill, he ordered her to take a pelvic exam. The result was terminal cancer that had spread throughout her body. Surgery was not an option for her, so she kept her illness a secret and would not confide in her friends and family.

Lola's second husband was obviously glad when she passed on, for he had enjoyed himself off her wealth; now he had it all. He married another woman three months after Lola was buried.

Lola made no will for her family, and she had no children. She did not give her second husband a prenuptial agreement. He inherited all her acres and acres of land left to her by her first husband Leland, his rented houses, and Lola's share in Papa's estate. It was on her death bed that she was able to speak about some things she wanted her sisters to have, but it was never entered into court records. Besides, her husband would hear none of it. He didn't give her family anything by which to remember their sister Lola because he also thought that from the way Lola talked about her family, they didn't deserve anything from her. Lola's family would hear nothing from her second husband, and they told him he had no right to the property Papa gave him. Lola was blamed for this terrible mistake she made. Nothing kept her husband from inheriting all her property. Her greedy husband developed Alzheimer's disease and passed away soon after Lola's death; his new wife is living well off Lola's wealth.

Ed had no means of income, and what little money he had was spent on whisky for himself and food for Mirah. She never stayed in the trailer with Ed, so she traveled back and forth from where she lived across the state line to visit Ed at least once or twice a month and tried to help him eat his meals and keep himself well. He wore a hearing aid, and when he had it turned down low, it was difficult for him to hear anyone knocking so he could open the door. But the day Mirah stopped by; it wasn't the hearing aid that kept him from answering the door.

When Mirah did not get an answer from Ed, she pushed the door open and found her way into the bedroom. She was shocked at what she saw. Ed had suffered a fatal heart attack and was lying stiff on the floor. Much to her surprise, he had been dead about two or three days.

The family was very sad and sorry that Ed had passed on. He didn't suffer long, but he had no understanding that he even had a heart condition. No one ever bothered to take the time to carry him to see a doctor. His brothers and sisters had all left him there on Papa's land to live out his days in destitution and sorrow. He was at peace now.

After Ed passed away, Mirah moved into her new brick low income house across the state border. She gathered all her belongings that Ed was keeping for her and moved them into her house. She visited the rest of her sisters at last, trying to keep in touch with the family.

Ed's sisters could tell that Van and Hugh took Ed's death very sadly. Van was able to stay sober a few hours for Ed's funeral, but as soon as the family had laid Ed to rest, Van and his old cronies took off to the juke joints and got themselves drunk.

Van had not changed, but he kept his job in the shipyard doing janitorial work. Each time he drank whisky, he suffered such terrible pain in the head that he was left groggy for days after his hangover had disappeared.

Once when Van could not quell the headaches, Hugh took him to the hospital. After the doctors examined him, he was diagnosed with a brain tumor. He was rushed into surgery and given anesthesia, but he never regained consciousness. A few days later, he died peacefully. His only assessed value was a share in the family's property, which went back to Papa's estate after he passed. His car was taken from him by a woman acquaintance, and she would not release it to the family. The government gave him an honorable funeral and burial plot although he was an army deserter. The United States flag was given to his brother Hugh.

Hugh missed his brothers and sisters after they passed on, being he was the oldest child Mama and Papa had. He had become so feeble that he was unable to keep a steady job. He stayed to himself most of the time, trying to get used to the various medications he needed to take for his uncontrollable diabetes and heart ailment. He led a quiet life, now, and his children remained close by and took good care of him. The only time Greta or Ginger saw their brother Hugh was when he took a notion to visit them during the weekends and holidays. Other than that, he never left home much, and hardly ever attended church.

Once when his daughter Evie visited him, she became very concerned about his health and whether or not he had suffered a slight heart attack. Not knowing what he was suffering from, she took him to the hospital to get an exam. The doctor discovered he had indeed suffered a slight heart attack and was kept under observation for several days. Before he could leave the hospital, he suffered a fatal heart attack and never returned home. He, too, passed away quickly and unafraid, with his daughter Evie at his bedside. His children grieved painfully for him, but they knew he was at rest.

No one was prepared for the shocking tragedy that Greta suffered. She had lived in her new home no more than seven or eight years before she had a new grandbaby girl and was babysitting her and working with her son in his construction business. Her life was just great, for she still loved her gardening, her work in the school cafeteria, and being a wonderful church lady.

Greta suffered a heart attack and was ordered to take bed rest and was given a special diet. She had no idea of the seriousness of her heart attack and spent little time remembering how ill she had been. Greta's doctor told her to take daily walks and eat healthy foods so she could stay active. She followed her doctor's orders and tried to keep as healthy as possible for the rest of her life.

Each Sunday after she went to church and ate her dinner, she took short walks. One Sunday when she was walking in the park, a sudden pain pierced her chest and threw her to the ground. Unfortunately, she did not take identification with her, so she lay there unable to move without anyone knowing who she was or what had happened to her. Someone in the park called for the ambulance that took her to the hospital, where she was pronounced dead.

After Greta did not return home for hours, her daughter, Gena, called the police to ask if anyone reported a lady who had been walking in the park. When they responded, after checking records to see who had been reported, they told Gena that a woman who had died while walking in the park was taken to the coroner's office. Gena was asked to come in and identify the body.

It was hard for Brownese when her sister Greta came to such a tragic end. She was always loved by everyone in the family, especially Brownese. Greta was a sweet, outgoing person and would openly share her goodness with anyone who came near her. Greta loved all her sisters and enjoyed being around them.

Brownese launched her professional career, married, and left the United States to live in Europe for several years. Her two children, who were born abroad, had barely reached school age when she and her husband returned to this country. She and her family settled on the west coast where she was a college professor until she retied.

As the years progressed and Ginger continued to work menial jobs, she became less and less competent to care for herself. She moved into a senior facility and joined various senior organizations sponsored by the Council on Aging. At that facility she was able to go sightseeing and take shopping trips.

The results of the gunshot injury to Ginger's head became worse. Many times while driving she continued to get disoriented, and even to get lost several times, ending up in a large city area where she couldn't recognize where she was and didn't know anyone. The condition gradually grew worse and further threatened her ability to care for herself, or even to walk. She had long been ordered to stop driving her automobile and was no longer issued a driver's license. Then she took to riding public transportation but could not recognize which bus would take her home.

Ginger was attacked with a second spell of advanced dementia, which confined her to a nursing home for over six months. During that time, she was unable to walk or to feed herself. Each day she struggled to regain her strength, but the onset of this terrible disease had all but given her family hope for expecting her life any other way. But she did get better, reminding her niece and nephew that she's a "tough old bird." She uses a walker when she goes to church or shopping once or twice a month. She also learned to feed herself again, hold a good conversation, and recognize her friends she comes in contact with. Her family wishes her well and hopes her health continues to improve.

Mirah has become Ginger's closest friend. She visits Ginger and takes her a lot of cheer. Whenever Gina tells Ginger that Mirah is coming for a visit, Ginger dresses in her nice clothes and waits for her to arrive. Sometimes she goes home with Mirah and stays for two or three weeks. The two of them confide in each other and talk a lot about what's going on in town and at church.

Mirah lives alone in her own home now. She keeps herself busy going to church twice a week and doing community activities with her friends. She maintains her living working a home-based business and doing catering work for her church and community.

Mirah's daughter, Maela, lives nearby and is especially watchful of her mom because she has the tendency to disappear for weeks without notice. It's to no one's surprise that Mirah escapes for several weeks during the holidays to visit the live-in family she kept for over twenty-five years, but she needs to let her daughter know where she is.

Mirah's son Tony has passed away, after suffering from several strokes.

Mirah's niece Liza picks Mirah up on weekends and keeps her in her home until after the weekend is over. Mirah stays "on the go" and never gets tired from being around friends and family. Although Mirah has retired from her live-in job, her year is not complete unless she visits the family she worked for at least twice a year, especially Thanksgiving and Christmas holidays.

The job of keeping up with the heirs to the family property is left up to Brownese. The property has been divided and recorded as two separate pieces of property. The south eastern section of the huge acreage has been sold to a local black contractor and the north eastern section planted in pine trees, which Brownese oversees.

It was difficult to escape the struggle and hardship this Negro rural southern family endured. Trying to make a living on the farm during the years following the Great Depression was both difficult and gruesome. The plow lands were wretched, and their inhabitants were forced to either survive on the land or escape to city slums. Each dawn promised new ways of stretching and shaping the farmland. But those who refused to stay on the land stumbled onto destructive pathways that linger on the edge of total demise.

"...The boundless forces of nature control our lives and compel us to follow the course we set for ourselves, however difficult the journey."

—The Author

About the Author

Ella O. Williams is an experienced writer of the social and moral life of African Americans. Her writing experience began during undergraduate work at Saint Paul's College. Later, while studying for a master's degree at New York University, Dr. Williams wrote many essays and scholarly papers about the life and literature of African Americans. Clark Atlanta University gave her the opportunity to delve more deeply into the study of African American culture. It was here where she studied African American literature and later wrote her dissertation: *The Harlem Renaissance: A Handbook*. For this publication, she achieved the Doctor of Arts degree in Humanities.

Dr. Williams taught communication, African American Literature, and Ethnic Humanities at Pierce College for over twenty-four years. During her tenure there, she began writing about the experiences of African American farmers during the end of the Great Depression. She has published several books. Among them is a most recent publication, *Strength to Carry On*. (Minerva Press, London, 1998).

Printed in the United States
80336LV00001B/1-75

9 781420 878417